Circle **K** Cycles

KAREN TEI YAMASHITA

COFFEE HOUSE PRESS

2001

COFFEE HOUSE PRESS is an independent nonprofit literary publisher supported in part by a grant provided by the Minnesota State Arts Board, through an appropriation by the Minnesota State Legislature, and in part by a grant from the National Endowment for the Arts. Support has also been provided by Athwin Foundation; the Bush Foundation; Elmer L. & Eleanor J. Andersen Foundation; Honeywell Foundation; James R. Thorpe Foundation; Lila Wallace-Reader's Digest Fund; McKnight Foundation; Patrick and Aimee Butler Family Foundation; Pentair, Inc.; The St. Paul Companies Foundation, Inc.; the law firm of Schwegman, Lundberg, Woessner & Kluth, P.A.; Star Tribune Foundation; the Target Foundation; West Group; and many individual donors. To you and our many readers across the country, we send our thanks for your continuing support.

COFFEE HOUSE PRESS books are available to the trade through our primary distributor, Consortium Book Sales & Distribution, 1045 Westgate Drive, Saint Paul, MN 55114. For personal orders, catalogs, or other information, write to: Coffee House Press, 27 North Fourth Street, Suite 400, Minneapolis, MN 55401.

Good books are brewing at coffeehousepress.org

LIBRARY OF CONGRESS CIP INFORMATION

Yamashita, Karen Tei, 1951–
    Circle K cycles / by Karen Tei Yamashita
        p. cm.
        ISBN 1-56689-108-6 (alk. paper)
    1. Brazilians--Japan--Fiction. 2 Japanese--Brazil--Fiction.
    3. Immigrants--Fiction. 4. Ethnicity--Fiction. 5. Japan--Fiction. I. Title.
    PS3575.A44 C57 2001
    813'.54--dc21

                                              00-065894

PRINTED IN CANADA

For Ryuta, Akiko, Rica, & Lei

ACKNOWLEDGMENTS
The Japan Foundation • Chubu University, Kasugai, Aichi
Ryuta and Akiko Imafuku • Momie Kishi
Jogi Enomura and Isabel Pereira • Celia Kimura and Keiji Yamanaka
Keijiro Suga • Gloria Delbim
Ted Hopes • Casey Krache • Ana Maria Seara
Chris Fischbach • Allan Kornblum • Linda Koutsky
Friends and acquaintances too numerous to name
in and connected to the Brazilian community in Japan
and as always Jane Tei, Jon, & Ronaldo

Contents

決

DEKASEGI STARTER DICTIONARY

dekasegi: verb meaning to work away from home; however, Brazilians and other migrant workers of Japanese descent have turned this word into a noun meaning: migrant laborer in Japan (spelled dekassegui in Portuguese)

empreiteira: contract employment company; middleman temp agency that hires laborers for factory work

gaijin: foreigner, outsider; more specifically, and sometimes negatively, non-Japanese

Nikkei: of Japanese ancestry or lineage; belonging to the Japanese tribe; however, some dictionaries translate this word to mean Japanese emigrant, or even Japanese American

nisei: second generation descendant of Japanese emigrants

mestiça: of mixed racial ancestry

san k: three k's: kitanai (dirty), kitsui (difficult), kigen (dangerous); used to describe work migrant laborers are forced to accept

sansei: third generation descendant of Japanese emigrants

saudade: longing, homesickness, nostalgia

Prologue: Purely Japanese

国

IN 1997, FOR SIX MONTHS FROM MARCH TO AUGUST, MY family and I lived in Seto, just outside of Nagoya in the prefecture of Aichi. Funded by a Japan Foundation Fellowship and sponsored by Ryuta Imafuku, then Professor of International Studies at Chubu University, I was there to meet and understand the Brazilian community living in Japan. During that time, I wrote a monthly travel journal for the internet website *CafeCreole*. In this book, those journal pieces are merged with works of fiction, in an effort to paint as varied and textured a portrait as possible of the life I saw and experienced during that time.

Just prior to this trip, I could think of three images that described my perceived relationship to Japan. The first is of the Butoh performer Kazuo Ohno dancing *La Argentina*. The second is of a car: a shiny sleek Mazda RX7. And the third is the presence as well as the voice of Maki Nomiya and her musical group *Pizzicato 5*. These are some of my favorite Japanese things, but also just some of my favorite things—reflecting a burnished and mature beauty, a graceful sense of line and movement, creative energy and play. They perhaps also reflect the cultural avant-garde and the technological and international nature of the relationship of the modern world to things Japanese.

In the more distant past, my relationship to Japan had not been tied to any pereconceived images other than the traditions of my Japanese American family. I first came to Japan in the early seventies on a kind of quest as a student, to study and travel. This was a period of activist movements across the world. In the U.S., the so-called Asian American Movement flowered with the quest for identity and the protest of the Vietnam War. I spent a year and a half in Japan, my main focus being to

research my family history, tracing my father's family back fourteen generations. My father's father came from a small village near Nakatsugawa in Gifu, his mother from Tokyo. My mother's parents both came from Matsumoto in Nagano. All of my grandparents immigrated to the Bay Area—San Francisco and Oakland—at the turn of the century. They were Meiji Japanese.

When I first arrived in Tokyo, I had short cropped hair, wire-rim glasses, flared pants, and a dark tan. I was a typical American sansei from California. As time passed, I exchanged my American clothing for Japanese, grew my hair, got contact lenses, and lost my tan. I also developed an intuitive grasp of mimicry. I pointed at my nose to indicate myself. I covered my mouth when I laughed. I held teacups with both hands. I kept my legs together when I sat. I used appropriately feminine Japanese. I passed.

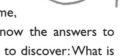

But every now and again, I would be questioned in a round-about way about my ancestry, about my parents and their parents until my story ended in Gifu, Tokyo, and Nagano. The questioner would then exclaim with surprise: *Ah, then you are a pure Japanese!* What could it mean to be a "pure Japanese"? I felt hurt and resentment. I came from a country where many people, including my own, had long struggled with the pain of racism and exclusion. Purity of race was not something I valued or believed to be important, and yet, in Japan, I was trying so hard to pass, to belong.

A few years later, in 1975, I received a fellowship to travel to Brazil. I was to study Japanese immigra-tion to that country. Brazil is home to over a million and a half Japanese immigrants and their descendants—the largest such population outside of Japan. That community has a long and fascinating history, and is a complex and varied society. But I knew very little of this when I first arrived; chance and intuition sent me to Brazil. I admit that I wanted to spend time in a warm, tropical, and sexy place, but perhaps I still wanted to know what being a pure Japanese might be. What was the essence, the thing that might survive assimilation and integration into a new cul-ture and society, the thing that tied communities in the North to those in the South and to the Far East?

Those questions, and more, kept me busy at my research for the next three years in Brazil. I wanted to know about the efforts of Japanese pioneers, their clearing of virgin forests, their extensive accomplish-ments in agriculture, their social struc-tures and political activity, their leisure, and their ideas. I wanted to know who these people were, why they came, 運命 what they believed. I wanted to know the answers to questions that might take a lifetime to discover: What is education? What is freedom? What is happiness?

In the meantime, I married a Brazilian archi-tect and artist, and our children were born in São Paulo. I continued to live in Brazil for almost nine years. We lived in the very busy center of the city on the fourteenth floor of a condominium high-rise. The street below was like a village unto itself, with small shops and businesses—the Portuguese bakery on the corner, the Korean grocery across the way, the stationery shop, the barber shop, the pool hall, the local bar, the Italian butchers, and the Japanese produce grocer—a cosmopolitan village.

Everyone called the Japanese grocer "o japonês." It was not unusual for me to ask o japonês to save me a cake of tofu or to put aside a half-dozen arti-

Empregos no Japão
Mais de 180 ofertas no Caderno de Classificados
páginas 1C e 8C
Aqui você encontra as melhores ofertas de imóveis
páginas 2 C

chokes for lunch. One morning, with my daughter in a stroller, I went down to shop on the street, stopping at all the usual places. O japonês decided to take up a conversation with me to sat-

isfy his curiosity. He was an issei, immigrated to Brazil in the thirties. His children were nisei. I told him that I was sansei. It had been a long time since anyone had wanted to trace my roots, but since he insisted, I took him back to Japan, to Gifu, Tokyo, and to Nagano. Yes, I was, without diversions of lineage, pure Japanese. I remember his reaction: "Ah," he exclaimed with a mixture of shock and disbelief, "how we become so different by the third generation!" as if I, by some accelerated Darwinian law of evolution, represented a strange and curious transformation. Brazil is a warm and friendly place; it is hard to be resentful toward anyone, and his was a reaction full of honesty and innocence. I remember feeling happy to laugh.

In 1984, we moved as a family from Brazil to Los Angeles. Through the experiences of my husband and children, I found myself immigrating back to my own country and into that great urban cosmopolitan cauldron of tremendous energy and ferment that is Los Angeles. We were a part of this change: immigrants, migrants, exiles, tourists, dekasegi, refugees, visitors, aliens, strangers, travelers all in search of work, education, new opportunities. As we crossed the border from south to north, we were also aware of a new movement of Japanese Brazilians making their way west to Japan to find work to support their families through yet another Brazilian economic slump.

In 1990, the Japanese government had passed a law to allow nisei and sansei to acquire visas to perform unskilled labor in Japan. At the same time, this law more strictly prohibited work by other foreign workers considered illegal aliens. Both government and business hoped to find a way to replenish the loss of unskilled factory labor, but in so doing to also replace non-Japanese foreign workers with the more familiar faces of Japanese descendants who should, it was thought, integrate more easily into Japanese life and society. In short, it was a solution probably well-intentioned but perhaps purely in favor of race.

Since 1990 a growing number of Japanese Brazilians and their families have migrated to Japan as contract

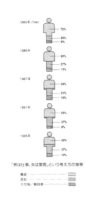

laborers to work in the myriad parts and subparts factories that support the products of companies like Toyota, Mitsubishi, Yamaha, Sony, Subaru, Sanyo, and Suzuki. They have also come to work in civil construction, food processing, health care, and to work as guards, hostesses, and golf caddies. These migrant workers have been named *dekasegi*, a term used to refer to workers who leave their homes, usually to work in factories in distant cities, to support their families. An estimated 200,000 Brazilian dekasegi now reside in Japan representing perhaps as much as thirteen percent of the Japanese Brazilian community at home.

As the first decade of the dekasegi comes to a close, one marvels at the resourcefulness and energy of these people. They have rapidly built small businesses: services such as educational programs, child care facilities, documentation and legal services, and associations and networks of every kind including soccer teams, internet cafes, and samba schools. The creation of community, in this sense, points to a new phase in the migration in which many are choosing to settle with their families in Japan. Every day, Brazilian consulates are filled with Brazilians needing documentation for marriages, divorces, and the birth of children in Japan. Dekasegi are known to work long hours, six, even seven-day weeks, taking on overtime without holidays for months on end. Many have or may return to Brazil with their savings to start businesses or to buy property. While some may succeed in reestablishing their lives in Brazil, many return to Japan, having lost their investments or their ability to reintegrate into Brazilian life. Although Japanese may regret their dependence on migrant labor and the disruption by foreigners of a homogeneous society, a dynamic bridge of migration between Brazil and Japan has nevertheless been established over which many travel constantly to sustain their lives and families in two homes.

I return to my three images: Kazuo Ohno, the RX7, and Pizzicato 5—things old and new, daring, innovative, creative, international, full of humor, traveling fearlessly. Purely Japanese. In a similar vein, I am aware that I should now add a fourth image, something to encompass the brave new Brazilian world experienced within Japan. For the moment I have no singular image but rather a range of images and stories contained within the following pages. In any case, how could any one image represent the lives and experiences of so many who have become so different and yet so purely Japanese?

March: Backache

体

I HAVE A BACKACHE. THIS IS AN OLD COMPLAINT, a secretarial one caused by years of pincering phone receivers between my ear and shoulder, along with excessive sitting and typing, further exacerbated by childhood scoliosis and little exercise. Sitting for long periods without back support on the floor may now also contribute to this discomfort. Finding some relief in the horizontal on a tatami floor under blankets or kotatsu, I doze off. The world becomes a great sleeping spine, and I have been dreaming. In my dream, my spine stretches out as a long bridge, traversing a great space.

There is the memory of the flight from LAX to Narita. Varig flight RG836. We join the spine of a great Boeing 747, its articulating vertebrae already constructed by several hundred dekasegi, businesspersons, and tourists whose travel has originated in São Paulo, Brazil.

KAREN TEI YAMASHITA

In Los Angeles, we are the last to fill in the remaining seats down the long backbone of this great flying whale.

Seats in airplanes are always too high for me; my legs dangle, my knees ache. The backrest is also too tall; it presses my head forward awkwardly. I do not participate in the medium American height. Is it an international standard? How many on the plane are participants? Surely, our bones will pay for this.

Our travel through space and altitudes is a continuum of digital dots on a flight monitor, precisely mapped, pushing through the same air, flight after flight. The compression of the cabin seals our hearing, and we slip through dreams and waking, glancing occasionally at the continuous American movies flickering endlessly in the dark. By the time we reach Narita, we will see four American movies; this means that the passengers from São Paulo have already seen four others. Twenty-four hours of travel and eight representations of Hollywood. We eye our watches for the time left behind, trying to match, yet hoping to forget, our physical clocks. Nevertheless, we arrive the next day.

The bullet train is an even longer spinal thing, an articulating steel serpent, dividing an old Japan from a new. Now we join the Japanese traveling population, each person with extended travel plans, starting from the farthest northern corners of snowy Hokkaido, tunneling through

15

on private trains and subways, taxis, buses, and ferries off Sado Island, toward palm trees in Kyushu. This is not a single spine but a great multiple dragon. Still, the Shinkansen is the fastest thing going.

We are instructed to sit on the right side of this spine in order to see Fujisan. I fit in these seats; my legs do not dangle. Relaxing into the comfort of another standard, some of us sleep and never see the sleeping volcano. At 200 kilometers per hour, Fujisan is in view for a full ten minutes, as we traverse 33 kilometers of its foothills. Travel on the Shinkansen is more precise than air travel: to the very second, it makes a cushioned stop like a soft sneeze. 11:22:00. Nagoya.

Settled in Seto, outside Nagoya, we have rented a car, a silver four-door Subaru coupe, vintage 1987. We apply a green and yellow arrow-like sticker to the backside of the car to indicate we are new drivers. We meet another Brazilian family using the same sticker on their car, but they've kept it there for three years now. Green and yellow: the colors of the Brazilian flag. *Honk if you are Brazilian. Cuidado! Brazilians in car.* Careful, these guys get confused; they're not used to this new spine where the

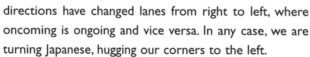

directions have changed lanes from right to left, where oncoming is ongoing and vice versa. In any case, we are turning Japanese, hugging our corners to the left.

Our friend Ryuta shows us the way from his house to our house. There is a Circle K convenience store on every corner. Four Circle Ks. To go to Ryuta's house, make a left turn at every Circle K. To go home, make a right turn at every Circle K. We are circling Ks. This is a joke about my name, Karen. Kon-binis. Open twenty-four hours. Climate controlled 365 days of the

year. What do we need? Eggs, yogurt, musubi, nori, or napa? Toothpaste or clothespins? A copy of my manuscript? Pornographic manga? Extra cash? We can even pay our phone, gas, and electric bills here. In this land of minimal spaces, the kon-bini is an extension of our rented space: our personal refrigerator, bathroom cabinet, office, library, and banking service. The routine of our lives sends us out circling Ks, no matter the hour, along a lighted path between my home and your home in my car.

E-mail. Internet. Connect. *Sorry, your modem is busy or is not connected. Please check settings for proper connection.* Click help. *The Internet Wizard will connect you. Sorry. Please call* MSN *Member Services Technical Help. 044-965-0196.* Type in AT&F in Advanced Settings. Type in S56=144 space S27=48. *The access number you have dialed is invalid. Please wait. Searching for baud rate for current access number. 9600. Welcome to CompuServe Member Services. $9.95 per month for 5 hours. Free trial period first month. However, surcharges from your site in Japan will be 35 yen per*

16

minute. (That's $20 an hour!) *Are you sure you wish to disconnect?* Try the Japanese software version. Can you read the katakana? Kyanseru. Herupu. From my modem to your modem. From my computer to your computer. Hardware vertebrae. Cable nerves. KDD. AT&T. My back hurts. We are not connected.

Occasionally we telephone out of desperation. On the other side, they answer: *Do you know what time it is? We are seventeen hours behind you! We need our sleep. Is this any time to call?* We are talking at the same time, but my time is not your time.

I can see the kanji, hiragana, and katakana gathering. They run down the page delicately, right to left. Now they also seem to run across the page left to right. Romaji jumps out at you. You piece your recognition together like reading abstract art. That looks like a cow. That looks like a violin. Hey, this is the gas bill! And this flyer: Pi-za. They deliver. Benri Japan. Ou, this is a flyer for sexy videos! That is, you can tell by the nude photos, but read it: bi-de-o. You don't get the girl in the flyer; you get the video of her. Kinky sexist Japan. Traveling my spine, from my tongue to my pubis, a sentient road, a sentient border. I need a massage.

My back aches. It is longer than it should be, expanded geographically. It is shorter than it should be, compressed and digitized. It is a great abstraction, a vertebrae of pidgin utterances in which I connect to the message maybe twenty-five percent of the time. It is multiple and reversible, disconnected yet utterly connected, timeless and long-suffering and infinitely sensitive. It is border and frontier. It is both vehicle and passenger. Conveyance and traveler. It is a bridge and a beast of burden. It is my back.

所定給付日数				（平成7年4月1日以降の離職者対象）	
被保険者であった期間 ／ 離職した日の年齢	1年未満	1年以上5年未満	5年以上10年未満	10年以上20年未満	20年以上
30歳未満	90日		90日	90日	180日
30歳以上45歳未満		90日	90日	180日	210日
45歳以上60歳未満		180日	210日	240日	300日
60歳以上65歳未満		240日		300日	

KAREN TEI YAMASHITA

整理整頓
MAINTAIN ORDER
MANTENHA A ORDEM

What If Miss Nikkei Were God(dess)?

者

MARCH AGAIN ALREADY. IMAGINE. ANOTHER MARCH, another year. Dekasegi are always counting the years like birthdays. For Miss Hamamatsu, this was year 3. She arrived in March on her fifteenth birthday, by most standards a fully formed woman. Blame it—womanhood, her full hips and breasts—on her Italian blood. Okay, blame her large dark eyes and her elegant nose on the Italians too. But the long silky black hair, the high cheekbones, the Shiseido perfect skin—blame that on the Japanese. She was that stunning mixture of Euro and Asian that feeds the filmic imagination. Her features represented the full measure of occidental beauty, all gracefully accented in the exotic. To top it off, she carried these Venus-like qualities with an easy Brazilian

KAREN TEI YAMASHITA

charm, as if the sun anointed her naked body, the sands and spume kissed her heels, her smile sparkled for everyone, and all of this in the middle of the industrial city, Hamamatsu, known as the home of Yamaha and Suzuki. Pianos and motorcycles. It all made perfect sense, for in Hamamatsu, among Brazilians who labored to produce those keyboards and racing monsters, and who likewise judged this contest of representative beauty at the local disco, she was known as Miss Hamamatsu '96. High priestess of music and speed.

栄光

But that was last year, and here she was, still at the same job, making multiple copies of Brazilian television shows for video rental distribution. The room where she worked was tucked away behind two storage rooms, warehouses for boxes of imported Brazilian products. To get to this back room, you had to negotiate a constantly changing maze around walled cartons of Cica tomato paste, hearts of palm, Knorr chicken soup cubes, Nestlé's sweetened condensed milk, Kimura polvilho, and Sadia gelatin. The video thing was a somewhat clandestine operation, but no one seemed to be too concerned about it. The police probably knew about it, but they would only investigate if a formal complaint were made, and who was going to complain about copyright violations of television shows half the globe away? The Japanese police wouldn't even know where to start. Who was Jô Soares to them? Or the Corinthians? *Fantástico?*

Still, Miss Hamamatsu '96, staring at walls stacked to the ceiling with JVC video recorders, dreamed of working somewhere else, in the open, in an office that had a window at least and young men passing to and fro who would of course turn their heads to appreciate her beauty. Such a waste, but then again, it was better than working in a factory, having to wear those ugly blue uniforms, subjecting her hands and nails to dirt and grease from machinery, bending over inspection lines of aluminum parts, minute after minute, hour after hour, day after day. This was work her poor mother had to do. She had been spared such a fate, but she would make it up to her family one day.

She was literally walled in by JVC recorders, 150 of them stacked in precarious towers of 10, side by side, a spaghetti of cables and electric cords snaking along the floor. In addition, scattered TV monitors of different shapes and sizes were lodged in between and on top of the VCRs, all flashing several different or identical shows. After two years of this, except for having to read the show titles on the tapes, she could probably perform her task in the dark, plopping fifty tapes into fifty VCRs at a time and hitting all the record buttons. Between recording functions, she was busy rewinding tapes, packing them for shipment, or slapping new labels over the old ones from a ticker tape of show titles run off a word processor / inkjet printer system. Used video cassettes got recycled over and over, and boxes of them were stacked everywhere. By the end of the week, last week's shows had to be reproduced from masters, categorized, and separated for distribution. She had no idea how many stores rented these videos, but she assumed they must take these copies and make more of their own. Some dekasegi in Kyushu was probably watching a fuzzy version of his team's winning penalty kick. Was it a goal or wasn't it? Home was a copy of a copy of a copy of a copy, further away than she could imagine.

At the moment, the blonde spectacle of Xuxa, a live Brazilian Barbie doll in a silver miniskirt and matching boots, bounced around a dozen of her prepubescent mini-replica Xuxettes. Like other girls her age, Miss Hamamatsu had grown up with the Xuxa Show, dreamed of being a Xuxette. She mimed the Xuxette routine on the small square of available floor space. One, two and kick and, three, four and turn, and . . . Miss Hamamatsu, like Xuxa, was a natural, and of course she loved little children. The Japanese had nothing like Xuxa. Miss Hamamatsu imagined she could bring this phenomenon to Japan as a measure of friendship. She would have Japanese and Brazilian children on her show, her little princes and princesses, talk to all the children out there, make heartfelt speeches about being kind to foreigners, bring those poor little kids who suffered from ijime[1] onto her program and make everyone feel sorry for them. If things were going to change in the world, they would change because of children. That was going to be her message. The show was over. Stop. Eject.

Stop. Eject. Stop. Eject. Stop. Eject. Stop. Eject. Stop. Eject. Stop. Eject. Stop. Eject. . . .

Jorginho popped his head in the door. "Oba!"

"Oi," she answered, grateful that he hadn't caught her dancing this time. Sometimes he would stand in the

doorway watching her until she noticed. It was really irritating, but she had to appreciate his appreciation. He was just about the only one around who noticed her in this dungeon, slaving among the tapes.

"Anything good?" he asked, rummaging through the week's titles. "How about saving me a copy of this?" He held up a tape.

She glanced at the title. *Chitãozinho e Xororó.* They were a popular country music pair everyone was listening to in Brazil.

"Leandro and Leonardo are coming to Japan," he nodded with inside knowledge about another musical pair. "I know the producers for the event. They're planning a tour in seven cities. They've got big backers, and they're going to rake it in."

"Are they coming to Hamamatsu?"

"If they don't, it'll be a big mistake. We're one of the biggest Brazilian communities. They'll probably get a sold-out event here. The fans will be clamoring."

"It won't matter if you're a fan or not. It'll be something to look forward to for a change," Miss Hamamatsu sighed.

Jorginho pointed to the tape of Chitãozinho and Xororó. "Don't worry, there'll be more. I'm going to see about bringing these guys to Japan too. Just let me make my contacts."

She smiled encouragingly. Jorginho had big plans. Well, they all had big plans. If you didn't have some kind of plan, you weren't a proper dekasegi. Then she pouted. "What about the Miss Nikkei Contest? Have you already abandoned that idea?"

"Worried?" he taunted her.

Ignoring him, she examined a master copy, copying down its title for duplication. It was Monday's episode of the current prime-time Globo novela: *O Rei do Gado.* It had arrived on a Varig flight that morning in a suitcase with other copies. She was possibly the first  person living in Japan to see that episode. She had work to do. "It's time to watch my novela," she announced. "Don't you have work to do?"

"Oh my dear," he spoke affectionately to her. "If there's a Miss Nikkei in this world, it's you. There's not a day that passes that I don't think of you." He smacked her

21

[1] ridicule

a kiss. "We're going to get you out of this video hell and make a lot of money with that pretty face of yours. Speaking of pretty faces—" He presented her with a large envelope.

"The photos!" she exclaimed.

"Proofs," he corrected. "Look them over, and we'll decide which ones to reproduce."

She scanned the tiny representations of her face and body. There were luscious exposures of her full lips and eyes filled with desire. There were nude poses, poses in string bikinis, poses in miniskirts, jeans, fitted jersey dresses. It was enough to drive any man crazy.

"And I've got some good news," he started in with a bit of suspense. "I met this guy whose sister used to be a model. Well, she's not a model any longer. Had kids. Put on weight. She's maybe in her thirties now. She just got a divorce, and she's thinking of joining this brother in Japan, see? So I got him thinking that he could invest some of that money he's been saving in his sister and open up a modeling school."

"Is this for real?"

"He showed me her old photos. She was a real stunner. Worked all over. New York. Paris." He waved his hands toward those distant locations. "It would take someone like her who knows the ropes to make this happen. I went out with him this weekend to look for places to open shop. All she's got to do is put up a sign. All the girls from the Miss Hamamatsu contest will come running."

"Including Miss Hamamatsu herself." She did a mock model walk up to the VCRs and back.

"Girl." He shook his head. "All that Brazilian beauty. There's got to be a way. Japan has this tropical gold mine and doesn't even know it."

She looked at her watch. "Jorginho, really, I've got to do the Monday novelas, or I'm in trouble."

"How about it? Karaoke tonight?"

"Maybe. I'll let you know." She brushed him off while shoving in the tapes for *O Rei do Gado*. It was the story of two Italian immigrant families coming to Brazil at

the turn of the century. The Mezengas and the Berdinazzis. Antônio Fagundes plays the father Mezenga. Tarcísio Meira plays the father Berdinazzi. In the beginning they are friends with neighboring coffee farms. Then they get in a fight over the boundaries and become enemies. The son (played by Leonardo Bricio) and the daughter (played by Letícia Spiller) of the respective families fall in love, but of course it's a forbidden love, a Romeo and Juliet story.

The theme song was beautiful. She could sing the entire song. There were scenes filmed in Italy. And scenes of coffee plantations and farm life in Paraná in the early part of the century. It was all so romantic. She felt it was her story too, the story of her Italian side. Imagine. Her grandmother could have been Letícia Spiller. Miss Hamamatsu sank into the full sensation of the novela moment; it was one of the perks of her job.

☺

The second week in March, she was making copies of director Tizuka Yamazaki's film, *Gaijin.* "Tizuka will be in Japan next month," Jorginho said, always in the know. "She's going to travel around to decide on a site for the sequel, *Gaijin 2*. In the meantime, she'll drum up interest for the old movie and try to get some sponsors for the new project."

Miss Hamamatsu had never even seen the first *Gaijin*. The heroine played by Kyoko Tsukamoto can't marry the man she loves, so she gets on a ship headed for Brazil with another man she doesn't love and leaves Japan forever. Like *O Rei do Gado*, this story is set in about the same time period. Kyoko has a hard life in Brazil working in the fields of a coffee plantation where Antônio Fagundes, this time, plays an Italian overseer who feels compassion for Kyoko's difficulties. The husband she comes to Brazil with dies of typhoid fever. By now she has a kid, and she can't pay off her debts to get out of her contract, so she decides to flee the plantation in the middle of the night. Antônio Fagundes follows her on horseback, but in the end helps her to escape. At the end of the movie, they meet years later in São Paulo. He's a labor organizer, and she's raising her child. Miss Hamamatsu wept at the end. It was her story too. Her mother was Japanese; her father was Italian. Her mother could have been Kyoko Tsukamoto; her father Antônio Fagundes.

Jorginho continued, "I know the people involved in producing *Gaijin 2*. I'm going to talk to them and get them involved in the Miss Nikkei Contest. There's a way this can work for everyone. We'll attract every gorgeous Brazilian woman in Japan. Who knows who might turn up? The future face or faces of actresses for this new movie, of course." He paused to reassure her. "I'm thinking of you, my dear, of course, but they don't need to know that."

It all made curious sense. In the novela, *O Rei do Gado*, Leonardo Bricio and Letícia Spiller, despite their feuding families, marry and have a son. Then the novela jumps ahead several years, and Antônio Fagundes who played old man Mezenga in the first episodes loses 20 pounds in 2 weeks and returns to play the grandson, Bruno Mezenga, the man who becomes the King of

NAKAYAMA MIHO

Cattle. She imagined further episodes: the King of Cattle becomes involved in an even more impossible and forbidden love affair with a beautiful Japanese woman. She, Miss Hamamatsu, would be the love child of this forbidden love.

Jorginho was ebullient with his ideas that day. "This is going to be a high-class event with high-class sponsors. Guaranteed. I've been talking to the KDD telephone people, to Varig, JAL, the Banco do Brasil. Everyone's enthusiastic. This is exactly the kind of event they're interested in promoting."

"Have you set a date and a place?" she asked.

"I'm looking into the Act City Plaza concert hall. Leandro and Leonardo are going to be booked there, too." Jorginho made a motion in the direction of the city's center, a large phallic tower planted in a music complex built to celebrate Yamaha and its theme for Hamamatsu: The City of Music. The Japanese called it Akuto Shiti. While Yamaha probably had international pretensions for its music center, it probably hadn't thought about a country music group from Brazil, not to mention a Miss Nikkei Contest. There in full regalia and pomp and circumstance, Miss Nikkei would proclaim her reign.

Thus Miss Hamamatsu imagined herself crowned in a diamond tiara, gliding down the walkway in that grand auditorium, her jeweled gown and velvet cape trailing behind her. Everything would be golden and glittering, lights flashing, stereophonic music swelling.

Meanwhile, she plastered labels onto video copies of *Gaijin*. The copies were probably illegal, but shouldn't every dekasegi see this film? A romantic story based on our history.

"I just thought of something," Jorginho congratulated himself. "How about this? We get Antônio Fagundes and Kyoko Tsukamoto, the original actors in *Gaijin*, to be the judges in the Miss Nikkei contest. Can you believe it? Now all we need is the participation of a former Miss Brazil."

Miss Hamamatsu smiled. Imagine.

☺

The third week in March, Miss Hamamatsu was looking over the large head shots of herself in black and white.

"My God, you're photogenic," exclaimed Jorginho. "There's not a bad take in the entire batch."

"Except when I was making faces." She made a face.

"Even those are wonderful. Shows you have personality. There's an actress behind that gorgeous face." He patted her cheek affectionately.

"Now what?"

"Now we make up a portfolio. I'm going to print up a résumé for you."

She looked at him quizzically.

"I know. I know." He waved away her concerns.

"I'll have to make some of it up, but who's going to check up on all the marvelous work you've done in Brazil?" He winked. "You'll see how we impress them. Put it on letterhead. All very professional with a slick folder. We put together a bunch of small folders to give away, to send out into the marketplace, test the waters, you know, send to magazines and newspapers. Then we have a large portfolio to take to meetings."

"Jorginho, you know I give most of the money I make to my mother, poor thing, for expenses. She sends all her money to Brazil to take care of her mother and my little brother there. Sure, I'm saving something for myself, and every once in a while I really splurge, but what I'm trying to say is that I can't go to meetings without dressing up a little."

"That's why these photos are important. Maybe we can interest a clothing company to have you wear their line of clothing and of course get free clothing in exchange. I'm in touch with the exclusive importer of a Brazilian brand of lingerie. When they see these photos, you're going to be their bra and panty pinup girl."

"It's going to take more than lingerie to dress this girl."

"So, we start with the basics."

"And don't forget makeup and hair."

"No problem." Like a magician, he pulled out a magazine. "Here's the latest copy of *Nova,* just in."

She flipped through this Brazilian version of *Cosmopolitan.* There was an article on skin care and nutrition, on shaping the face with cosmetics and matching makeup to skin tone, on pedicures, on hair color, on the

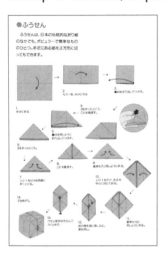

latest in Fall fashions (it would be autumn in Brazil), and on orgasms. She sighed. Being beautiful was a full-time job. How she would like to check into a bona fide beauty salon once in a blue moon. Brazilian women went to each other's houses. Her mother's friend Arlete did hair and nails. Her girlfriend Flávia did depilation and face masks. They shared cosmetics and exchanged clothing. If she stepped into one of those fancy Japanese places, there was no telling how she would come out. There were Nikkei girls who you could swear were Japanese. They spent their money on the Japanese styles, and their bodies fit into those hipless pants and dresses. She was longer in the torso and legs and wider in the hips and bust. Imported Brazilian clothing for an imported Brazilian body; it took some finances to keep up her looks.

Jorginho looked over her shoulder at the magazine's advertisements. "I had an inspiration this morning. All we need is a video camera."

"You want to tape me?" she asked in mock surprise.

"Better than that. For example, this lingerie importer. We could do an ad for their lingerie. A commercial. I know a guy who used to work for Globo TV in Rio. I could get him to do the camera work."

"But where are you going to place this commercial? On Japanese TV?"

"It's amazing I never thought of it." He put his arms up and looked around the room. "This is our mother lode. This is where it can all start!"

Miss Hamamatsu gave him her full smile but looked confused.

Jorginho pointed at the video tapes. "Like a trailer or intros, understand? Or we could slip our commercials in at the regular breaks. Can you imagine the kind of money we could make, not to mention the exposure? These videos go out to dekasegi all over Japan."

"Do dekasegi buy a lot of lingerie?"

"Okay, not just lingerie. How about jeans? You look sensational in jeans."

"Can you believe it?" She patted the Brazilian tag on the pocket. "This imported pair cost me ichi man yen."

Jorginho calculated 10,000 yen—about 80 dollars. His eyes wandered lovingly over her bottom as she bent over to retrieve used tapes. "No wait! How about meat? We're importing hundreds of tons of Australian beef into Japan every month. You could do a meat commercial. Wear a cowboy hat. Sing a country music tune

with a barbecue going on behind you. I'm not kidding. I know the owner of a meat distribution company. Leave it to me."

With the mention of beef, her mind wandered back into the continuing saga of *O Rei do Gado*. The first generation of Mezengas and Berdinazzis gradually die off.

The second generation sells the coffee farms, exchanging their inheritances for even bigger ventures. Mezenga becomes the King of Cattle and Berdinazzi becomes the Dairy King, and they still hate each other. Raul Cortês plays Berdinazzi, the Dairy King. Miss Hamamatsu thought he was perfect in his role, gradually growing old over the course of the novela. She thought about this incredible opportunity to pretend to be someone else for months and in full public TV view until practically everyone in Brazil knew even the most intimate things about this other you. Maybe being in a commercial wasn't the same thing, but imagine: she could become the Queen of Beef.

The fourth week in March, Jorginho said, "I think we've got a bite. I sent your photos to this magazine operation." He waved a shiny copy in the air.

She could see the pose of a woman in a string bikini, down on all fours, the most prominent part of her—her buttocks—pressed against the glossy surface of the magazine's cover.

Jorginho reassured her. "This is a high-class operation. Look at the quality of these photos, the quality of the paper. It's sophisticated stuff. And prominent exposure. They are doing big business not only with the dekasegi crowd here in Japan but in Brazil as well. After all, beautiful women are beautiful anywhere. I told them they should put some Japanese translations in the margins. Japanese men are crazy for Brazilian women. They could get this market as well. How about it? You could be the foldout in the next issue." He unzipped the crisp protective cellophane of the magazine and dropped the foldout from the slick pages. A woman, naked except for a cowboy hat and boots, hung there, a limp tribute to Brazilian country music no doubt, and yet, the Queen of Beef. The dekasegi girlfriend of the month.

Bruno Mezenga is unhappily married to the bitchy Sílvia Pfeiffer who is having an affair with a gigolo. In the meantime, Mezenga meets Luana played by Patrícia Pillar who is involved in the Movimento dos Sem Terra. She comes with a group of landless peasants and squats on Mezenga's land. Bruno Mezenga proves that his land is in use and that he's a good man, so Luana falls in love with him. It's true love. And besides, Patrícia Pillar is so rapturously beautiful even in jeans, without makeup, and playing an idealistic activist, he'd be stupid not to fall in love with her. The secret is that Luana is really a Berdinazzi and doesn't know it. Fate is at the crossroads.

さわるな
DO NOT TOUCH
NÃO TOQUE

KAREN TEI YAMASHITA

As a dekasegi, Miss Hamamatsu appreciated the message of the downtrodden, those without land. They had every right to take over land held by absentee landlords and make it productive. Was there no justice in this world? She would be the Japanese mestiça Patrícia Pillar, the righteous and beautiful Luana. She with other dekasegi would take over Japanese contract companies and production lines. One day she would meet a powerful and princely Japanese executive who would sympathize with her plight and fall madly in love with her. It would be a true but forbidden love and eventually, after many episodes, their love would bring two feuding families—Japanese and dekasegi Nikkei—together and change the world.

The naked Queen of Beef still flapped between the porn pages, and Jorginho continued. "Listen, it's a beginning. Everyone has to start somewhere. It's understandable why this magazine has really taken off. All these single dekasegi men are living in dorms with other men. All they see is other men, work double shifts and overtime round the clock. Girl, have you no pity? A life of drudgery. What have they got to look forward to? They miss their girlfriends. They don't get any action. If they go to discos, it's one woman to ten men. You women can pick and choose. When a beauty like you comes along, it's natural that we should want to spread the bounty around. It's just a photo. What's the harm of a little imagination?"

Miss Hamamatsu looked around at her video recorder world. All at the same time, 150 VCRs were making 150 copies. *O Rei do Gado* was on all the monitors, but at slightly different moments in the same episode. It was disconcerting to watch. Bruno Mezenga embraces Luana; they kiss passionately. Their theme music surrounds them as the romantic moment is caught from several angles. All the monitors stuttered this image in various stages like a singing round. Since this current novela was picking up popularity, it was necessary to make more and more copies. It was a big seller in all the stores. Next week, maybe all the dekasegi women would be watching this scene, and all the dekasegi men would be staring at the naked Queen of Beef. Imagine.

Jorginho replaced the centerfold. "Actually, the guys at this magazine are looking to expand their horizons. They're interested in exploring the video end of the business. This is in the future of course, but it's a marketing opportunity they'd be foolish not to take advantage of. I'm working on them to sell my idea about commercial inserts in video rentals. I think they're interested in investing in it, you know, as a start. You have to start somewhere."

Miss Hamamatsu followed the kisses around the room, copied from one VCR to the next, 150 times. The scene closed. *To be continued.* Then the credits came up. She ejected the master copy and inserted another with the next episode. "I guess you're right," she agreed. "I imagine you have to start somewhere."

"Of course they're going to invest in the Miss Nikkei Contest. Their investment will bring us over the top. Hey." He pulled her away from her work and caught her in an embrace. "I'm also planning a ballroom dance with Miss Nikkei and her entire court. It's going to be the event of the year!" he exclaimed. He took his queen in a precarious waltz around her electronic prison. "By the end of the year, my dear, we'll be dancing our first dance." He ended with an exaggerated bow and she with a grand flourish.

Then she hurried to push all the play / record buttons.

Jorginho paused to worship her. A moment of reverence and then the theme song. Miss Nikkei. She was the best of both worlds.

April: Circle Trash / Maru-Gomi

新

Saturday, February 22

We are introduced to the house we will rent in Seto. It is a two-story house built in the sixties, and one of three similar houses standing side by side. 2-20-3 Kohancho. Our friend Akiko initiates introductions to our surrounding neighbors. She has a gift for each neighbor and a very important question: Which days, at what time, where, and how must we dispose of our trash? I listen to the answers conscientiously; I want to be a good neighbor.

Monday, February 24

We rent a truck and go with friends, Akiko and Ryuta, to Gifu City. Akiko's parents are cleaning out a house in preparation for new construction. They are about to get rid of a washing machine, a refrigerator, a microwave, a television, tables and chairs, and futons, a precious trove of furniture and electro-domestic goods for our empty rental house in Seto.

KAREN TEI YAMASHITA

Wednesday, February 26, evening

Our neighbor, Mrs. Takahashi, comes over with a slick poster explaining in detail when and how to deal with our trash. The poster has pictures of four trash groups: trash to be burned, including plastic, paper, and kitchen garbage; recycled trash such as bottles, cans, and newspaper; another section for what seem to be ceramics and light bulbs; and finally a section for big trash, including bicycles and washing machines. She also offers us a package of yellow sacks for appropriate disposal. I understand that the clear yellow sacks are for "burnable" trash. Moeru-gomi. I must get my moeru-gomi out on Mondays and Thursdays at 8:30 A.M.

Thursday, February 27, morning

Our alarm alerts us at 8:25, but I have been awake already for at least an hour fumbling in the cold with the clock trying to decipher the time in the dark, worried that the trash truck will come and go without my moeru-gomi. We've left the trash at the door in readiness. The house is miserably cold at this hour; slipping out of futons is the last thing we want to do. I get dressed, struggle with my shoes at the door, and run out with our trash. I feel a sudden panic when I see no bags of trash at the street corner location previously indicated by Mrs. Takahashi, then relief as two yellow bags of hefty moeru-gomi appear about five meters to the left. Mission accomplished. I walk back thinking I will also see my neighbors in a similar and concerted rush to augment our small pile, but no one appears to notice my common sacrifice for community.

Friday, March 7

We receive a box of traditional sweets. The box is presented to us in a colorful paper bag with handles. It is wrapped in stylized rice paper, hiding the box itself—a sturdy cardboard construction pasted with more fine paper. Parting another layer of tissue, within, the box is segmented, each plastic partition bearing an individually wrapped confection. We slowly unwrap each confection which is in turn wrapped in a final edible wrapper. We pour tea. We chew slowly. Every bite must count. Meanwhile, we fold and flatten the seven or more inedible layers of wrapping gathering in a growing pile along with the candy's historic and sales brochures, plus packages of inedible desiccant. It is an odd lesson in economics. Packaging represents full employment. Our pile of waste represents layers upon layers of jobs. We can mince thoughts over the humidity of the climate or the cultural aspects of wrappings, and of the tea ceremony, but the welfare of the nation requires this.

Sunday, March 16

We visit a Brazilian family in their apartment near Tsurumae Park. They explain that Brazilians hardly have to buy anything upon arriving in Japan. Furnishings and warm clothing are usually handed down from other sojourners, but the greatest source of all is the trash. Lixo. That new three-part refrigerator, this bilingual VCR and television, that small oven, the kotatsu, the full-cycle washing machine, the telephone / fax machine: all in working condition; all lixo. There are also stories of incredible finds: an upright organ encased in polished cherry wood, entire computer systems, big-screen stereo televisions. Every neighborhood has a certain place and a certain night for its trash. You take your flashlight and bump into other gaijin scavenging.

The Japanese, the Brazilians say, would never do this. The Japanese don't want other people's old things. They are superstitious: used things bring bad luck. A new home needs new stuff. If you leave an apartment, you have to remove everything from it. Japanese don't want to rent a place with used appliances. It's often cheaper to dump your old stuff than to cart it to the next home. Space is at a premium; no American garage to tuck away the old TV. No room to store the winter futons or clothing; easier to trash them and buy another set next year.

Tuesday, April 1

We help a friend exchange apartments with another family in the same building. She's moving upstairs. The other family will move downstairs to the ground floor. The exchange is made so that their daughter, who is in a wheelchair, won't have to be carried up and down the stairs. The apartments are about equal in size: two $4\frac{1}{2}$ tatami bedrooms, kitchen, and bath. The stuff that's compressed into these spaces boggles the mind. The more we remove, the more there seems to be: appliances large and small, dishes and groceries, pots and pans, bedding and clothing, cleaning solutions and clothespins, toys and magazines. I bag an endless collection of recycled trash, plastic bags and paper sacks, bottles and old plastic margarine tubs, accumulated knick-knacks for some special project that never came about. My friend coordinates a growing pile of things she will abandon to the trash. Her elderly mother picks among these things and quietly retrieves this and that when her daughter is not looking.

Sunday, April 6

I meet with a man who is the kucho[1] of the residents of a complex of condominiums housing some 7,000 people, 2,000 of whom are Brazilian. He cites trash as one of the problems the condominiums face. Will the Brazilians cooperate with the new trash system? A questionnaire has been sent out to all the Brazilian occupants. An entire section is devoted to "problemas relacionados com o lixo." "Have you seen the notices in Portuguese regarding the correct disposal of trash?" "Do you use the appropriate sack to throw away trash?" "Do you throw away burnable trash and nonburnable trash on the appropriate days?" "Do you know where to throw your trash?" "Are you aware of how trash should be separated?" "What do you think is required to facilitate the collection of trash?" "Will you collaborate with the new rules for trash disposal in April?"

Tuesday, April 15

We offer to drive Brazilian friends to Osaka to pick up a car left behind by another friend returning to Brazil. Their own car has already been sent to the crusher. As Brazilians, we mourn the discarded car, which by other standards was still new and useful. However, Japan requires an expensive inspection, a shaken, that will cost at least $1,500, not to mention repairs to any systems that don't meet the standard. Another car can be bought for the cost of the shaken. We note the sticker dates indicating the shaken for the car picked up in Osaka; its years are numbered as well.

A Brazilian import / exporter has told me that he has tried to send old car parts to Brazil to be reassembled once there. It's an idea that quickly comes to mind: can't these old cars be useful elsewhere? The Brazilian government, to protect its own automotive industry, won't allow it. India, however, permits this, as does the Philippines. Cars are sawed in half, sent in containers, and welded together upon arrival.

[1] president

Saturday, April 19

Brazilian friends scout some prime areas known for valuable trash. These sites are usually near large condominium structures with hundreds of apartments and thousands of residents. We see a few boom boxes but nothing special. The good stuff has been picked over already.

We look up into ten-story structures, futons hanging over the balconies, T-shirts and underwear hung out to dry. Lots of Brazilians live here, but for a late Saturday afternoon, it's oddly quiet by Brazilian standards. People working zangyo. Overtime. People sleeping off the late shift. Their lives in Brazil may have been very different; they may have never worked a factory job before. Now they circle the three Ks. Kitanai. Kitsui. Kigen. Work designated as dirty, difficult, dangerous. A bank clerk presses metal into car bumpers. An engineer hangs pigs on hooks in a meat processing plant. A stationery store owner drives a trash truck. A fifteen-year-old boy mixes cement at a construction site. A grandmother solders tiny wires to electronic plates. They are the same people in Japan as they were in Brazil, but there are new and different uses for their lives. And if the bank clerk loses his fingers or the grandmother suffers a heart attack, there is another clerk with fingers, another grandmother with a heart.

We don't want any old boom boxes. We're looking for a VCR. We settle for a pair of old chairs.

Saturday, April 26

I sweep out my daughter's room on the second floor. It's the guest room with 6 tatamis and a tokonoma. She is collecting broken pieces of ceramics she finds in the dirt and streets all around Seto, an old and traditional center for ceramics and Chinaware. Seto-mono. The pieces are arranged across the mats and tokonoma like puzzle pieces and artifacts from an archaeological dig. Designs drawn in traditional blue, repetitive abstractions, fragments of kanji, wabi[1] / sabi[2]—all rest in the dappled light across the straw and wood—a beauty my daughter grasps at as if she can see the entire teacup, dish, or vase in its original luster and usefulness. The beauty of trash.

In any case, I scoop it all up, save it in a plastic sack, and continue to sweep.

---

[1] taste for simple and quiet   [2] patina, antique, profound simplicity

Three Marias

社

WHEN ZÉ MARIA fiRST ARRIVED IN JAPAN HE thought: What Brazilian could stand the cold of this country? But they all said: Thank God it's April. By the end of this month the weather should turn. Then we get May, and look forward to that, because May is the only decent month in the year, unless it rains. Even after seven years, who could get used to this cold? Take some Carioca, a native of Rio, who never owned a wool coat

until coming to Japan. My God, the only thing a Carioca knows about wool is that it comes from sheep.

After seven years, Zé Maria thought: This dekasegi thing, it's all the same ball of wax. It's one mafia. The contract companies, the government, business, banks, even those agencies that are supposed to give assistance. It's all the same thing. One great yakuza. If

you think you're in control of your destiny, look again. Not that the yakuza is involved. Maybe they are. Maybe they aren't. And who are *they* anyway? What does it matter? Who needs the yakuza with a setup like this?

LOOK, IT'S A SEVEN POINT PROGRAM:

① GOVERNMENT AND BUSINESS. Government, pressed by Big Business, created a law to let Japanese descendants into the country to work in Japanese factories. The law was just a formality. Japan had a long-range plan, a 100-year plan. Looked into a crystal ball and saw the future. Saw the A-bomb hit Hiroshima and, to save the race, sent away colonies of their people to South America. Like sending people to the moon. Seventy years later, call them all back to do the work of the nation.

② CONTRACT EMPLOYMENT COMPANIES (EMPREITEIRAS). There's another law that says that Empreiteiras that sell human labor are illegal. Illegal! But businesses don't want the trouble of hiring dekasegi. So Government, controlled by Business, looks the other way. Let the bastards in to work!

③ TRAVEL AGENCIES. Travel Agencies in Brazil act as fronts for Empreiteiras and provide documentation, contacts, and airfare to dekasegi. It's all about a handshake and making the $tutu$.

④ BANKS. When a dekasegi gets to Japan, he saves all his money to send home by remittance through the Banks. Banco do Brasil. Banco do Estado. Put it all together, it's 2 billion dollars a year, my friend! Business is Business.

⑤ DISPATCHING SERVICE AGENCIES. When the dekasegi needs to renew his visa, he pays a fee to the Empreiteira for this service, or he goes to an Agency. This Agency may say they do the work for free, for the good of the people, but behind the charity is funding from one of the three major Telephone Companies. But get this, paperwork in Japan is easy. Any fool can fill in these forms in Romaji.[1] Ah no. The Brazilian is an accommodating animal. Everyone is working the system riding on his shoulders.

⑥ TELEPHONE COMPANIES. You pick and choose: KDD, ITJ, IDC. In order to talk to his mother on the weekends, the dekasegi decides he'd better rent the telephone service from the Agency. At $2.00 a minute and with that mountain of saudades,[2] it's going to cost him a day of his sweat at least.

⑦ NEWSPAPERS. A dekasegi gets his news by reading one of four Brazilian newspapers. He wants to know if the economy in Brazil is favorable for returning. The Newspaper has articles of dekasegi success stories, and of bloody crimes and political scandals back home. Since the Newspaper is supported by ads paid for by Empreiteiras, Travel Agencies, Banks, Dispatching Service Agencies, and Telephone Companies, it will *always* be favorable to return *and* it will *never* be favorable.

☺

Right or wrong? With a program like this, what's a dekasegi got to lose but his life while everyone else makes money off his disgrace. Desgraça yes, but coitado[3] no. No dekasegi is a poor victim. After all, every dekasegi knows this wheel of life. Problem is, most only know it on the inside. They're running around in it, round the clock, working double shifts and zangyo,[4] saving the money or sending it all home. Open your eyes! Down deep, dekasegi are a bunch of tricksters. Every once in a while, there's a dekasegi who tries to step off the wheel, tries to run the program rather than run with it. Like Zé Maria Fukuyama.

Zé Maria began his career as a dekasegi back in Brazil on a Saturday in a bar, drinking Brahma with his buddies. They were doing the rounds and talking about how hard it was to make a living. Someone pointed out that he was the only one among them who had a chance. Wasn't his grandfather Japanese? Why shouldn't

---

[1] Roman letters   [2] longing, homesickness, nostalgia
[3] poor, miserable fellow   [4] overtime

34

he make use of his genealogical tree? Being Japanese must be good for something, especially if it's for money.

On the following Monday he wandered into one of the thirty travel agencies in Brazil set up to catch fools like him. These places are fronts for the contract companies who can't legally peddle their promises in Brazil. To get a one-year visa, you have to buy a round-trip ticket that you never use. What dekasegi can make his fortune in one year? For dekasegi, a $1,600 ticket goes for $3,500. That's the price. Take it or leave it. You're going to be making so much money, they assure you. You can pay it back easily on overtime alone.

What did he know? Zé Maria took the trip. He had his passport, his visa, and a heap of promises—like he was going to work in a reputable company called Suri Emu (hadn't he heard of it?—3M), work a clean cushy job, have a nice apartment with a room all to himself, none of this 3K Kitanai Kitsui Kigen[5] stuff. 3M all the way. Arriving in Japan, the contract company sent someone to pick him up, put him up with seven other men in a two-room apartment in a pre-fab tin box bungalow. The contract company took his passport as a guarantee that he'd complete his contract to work and

pay up his debts—his airfare, his housing, and the money they'd invested in him.

Then he started his job: an assembly line position. Suri Emu? Our contract company doesn't work with them. Who told him that? No, his job was to get on his knees and screw in some part to another part. He performed this task over and over again in two eight-hour shifts. His knees burned. His back ached. It

was relentless. He complained to the supervisor that he could do his job better if he had a table to work on. The supervisor said something he didn't understand. He complained to the contract company rep who told him to be patient. He just got there; maybe they'd get him another job. He also wanted to complain that he'd been promised an apartment with his own room, but he was too tired every night to notice the bodies heaped about on the tatami.

The following week, the supervisor motioned to Zé Maria to follow him to another work station, and demonstrated his new job, which was to drill and cut aluminum pieces. There were signs all over the machine, but he couldn't read them. Porra![6] The only thing he could understand that the Japanese said was, "Okay?" He never wanted to get on his knees again and see another screw, so he answered, "Okay. Okay."

---

[5] dirty, difficult, dangerous   [6] literally semen, sperm; exclamation: damn!

Two weeks later, he was falling asleep at his job. The men who shared his room snored. He was losing sleep and weight. Instead of drilling when he should drill, he brought down the guillotine to cut. His fingers were in the way. His blood splattered everywhere. What a mess! Workers down the line who saw his fingers on the belt

整理整頓

mixed in with the aluminum parts and blood screamed, but the shock of the event left him without a voice.

They put his fingers in a plastic bag and whisked him off to the hospital, did microsurgery on the fingers and saved 2 out of the 5. When it came time to pay the hospital bills, they told him he didn't have insurance, that the factory had graciously offered to pay his bills, after which he was promptly fired. In the meantime, the contract company was holding his passport until he paid his debts. Up to now, you'd think this Zé Maria was some dumb fool, but he hadn't yet met the first of three Marias.

☺

Maria da Conceição handed him her card. "At your service," she practically saluted him. "Now let's get down to business. Don't think your situation is the first of its kind. No No. Not at all. Losing fingers is the number one accident among dekasegi. You're lucky. You didn't lose your arm or leg or your eye. My organization was created exactly to help cases like yours. What we've discovered is that the average dekasegi doesn't know his or her rights. Our program is threefold: assistance, education, activism. First we are going to offer you assistance. In doing so, you have a responsibility to become educated about your case and your rights and the laws. This is absolutely essential. Foreign workers have rights protected by international law which are being completely ignored by Japanese businesses. That is where activism comes in. Once you are educated, you have a responsibility to call attention to injustice and to be vigilant in protecting the rights of others." This woman meant business; it was evident. She immediately went to work for him, got a disability settlement from the factory, got back salary for the days of work he missed, got penalty payments from the contract company that had failed to secure health benefits for him, got his passport away from them too, and got his job back.

What woman had ever done so much for the poor bastard? It had to be love. She was a saint. Zé Maria fell on his knees, cried to God for pity's sake, and worshipped her. Religious fervor can be a hard-on. He looked up into her radiance and had a vision. She fell on top of him and worked him into raw material. It was a dekasegi's wet dream. Who'd have thought he could be the recipient of so much left-ist passion? Of course he wasn't on the receiving end for long; she pulled him up and booted him out, booted him out into the wide world. It was a threefold program after all. Assisted and educated, he was all set to claim a piece of the action.

He got on his casework right away. Maria da Conceição was right. He wasn't the first or the last to lose his fingers. He had to make phone calls to families back home in Pirapora, Caraguatatuba, and Pirassununga, tell them their son or daughter or husband or wife was paralyzed from the waist down, was mentally ill, had committed suicide, was in jail for drugs, was desti-tute and sleeping in the streets. He had to pin down the institutions responsi-ble, hold the law up for abiding. He had to find money to support his work, sponsor benefit dances and events, pull money in at the door to keep the rent and the utilities paid. A year went by. He was an evangelist with a cause, working for the poor and downtrodden, for the little guy lost in a foreign country. Wasn't long before he figured out that he was one of the few to get to fold #3 of the program. He did-

n't fault the guy who died, but most dekasegi who got saved never even called him back to say thank you. Not a postcard, not a donation, not a single convert to a life of activism. No wonder Maria da Conceição went bananas. That's right. He was getting cynical.

Then, one day, an unusual case came up. Nobody wanted to touch it. It wasn't a clean case of victimization, but then, as he knew, none of them were. She was a dekasegi in jail. It wasn't drugs. It wasn't prostitution. The police had got-ten her for infraction of the labor law. She'd been doing business as a contract employment company, an empreiteira, selling out human labor for a fee. A dekasegi who was hired by an empreiteira wasn't any-thing new, but one who'd gone into business for herself, and a woman at that, now that was something rarer. He wanted to meet this woman. Name was Maria Madalena. But first he had to get her out.

He sent in a lawyer. More impor-tantly, he sent out a story to the newspapers. Who was Maria Madalena? A working woman trying to survive in Japan. So she'd been doing the work of an empreiteira, getting jobs for other dekasegi for a small fee. What of it? She made a small living for herself. What about the thou-sands of other contract companies owned by Japanese that hired thousands of workers and made billions of yen off the sweat of human labor? What was Maria Madalena's little venture in the middle of the bigger picture? Who cared about her cramped little office with a fax machine, on the second floor above a plastic food shop? Who'd she gotten jobs for? Dekasegi nobody wanted to hire: an old couple, hard of hearing—got them jobs packing lunches in a musubi operation; a dark-skinned man—got him a dishwashing job; people without legal documents—got them real jobs, no questions asked. She was a small fish taken out to show that the law was being enforced. What was she doing that the big fish weren't? Why weren't they sitting in jail with her? Was it because she was a foreigner? Were the Japanese the only ones who could break the law and get away with it?

Zé Maria was on a roll. He was going to move some mountains, or so he thought. He got his network to send letters of protest, writing to the newspapers, raising a big stink. Nobody wanted to deal with this issue because as it's been said, it's all one big mafia—the hand that feeds being the hand that packs a punch. As soon as this Maria Madalena thing got some press, someone must have said, "Bad news. Get the bitch outta jail."

So they took the cuffs off Maria Madalena and handed her over to her savior. Zé Maria wasn't prepared for the amount of woman packed into his mission. If his mission was to play ball with the big-time, Maria Madalena had the body, the breasts, the hips, and the presence of a woman who could bust a mission and then some. If he had known who she really was, he would have left her to her own devices. Maria Madalena looked over all the press coverage, wet her lips, watered her eyes, and smiled for the cameras as she emerged from prison. It was the triumph of justice. It was Zé Maria's downfall.

But unlike other dekasegi he'd gone to bat for, Maria Madalena was grateful, and she wasn't averse to showing how much. If he'd gone to heaven with Maria da Conceição, he went to hell with Maria Madalena.

She laughed at his threefold plan, but caressed his three missing fingers. Don't get her wrong, she said. She was grateful, but after an education like hers, activism was about working the system and beating the crooks at their own game. Her operation was small, but she was back, and she had no intention of stopping. Oh, she had learned her lesson, sure, and they would never catch her again. What Zé Maria didn't understand, as far as she was concerned, was what dekasegi really needed. They needed a dose of reality, a kick in the butt. Even if they knew their rights, why were they being shepherded around by Japanese empreiteiras? Her idea was to take the business out of Japanese hands. As a Brazilian empreiteira, what did

she do? Did she coddle dekasegi, tell them lies about their jobs, the money, the benefits? No! She told them the work was difficult, dirty, and dangerous, that they could lose their health, and even their lives, that if they didn't come here for this, then they'd better find a way to leave. Making money in Japan was no picnic. Did they want the job or not? Take it or leave it. Plenty of others in line who wanted work. She told them the truth; it hurt, but it made sense. A lot of them came back to thank her, thank her for the job and for making them see reality. And she made her money. It was more than Zé Maria could say for all his goodwill. He joined up.

Pretty soon, Zé Maria was running the fax machine and making phone calls, sitting dekasegi down and giving them a reality pill. He excelled at this because he could cite real examples, people he knew who were worse off, even dead. Think about it, he'd say. Look at my hand. He could point at his missing fingers. He was lucky. Will you be so lucky? You have to take charge of your life. You got your rights, but it's not a free ride.

Eventually some of them came back to thank him, thank him for busting their butts. He'd never thought that Brazilians could be so masochistic, but then he remembered how losing his fingers had made him an activist. Maria Madalena was right. He'd thought his genealogy was an easy ticket to money, but he was just another fool ready to get his fingers whacked off, look-

ing for sympathy. Brazilians were fools for the comfortable, wanted everything handed to them on a silver spoon. Here it was all chopsticks. Food kept falling off. How hungry could you get? Hungry enough to make it? Hungry enough to fight? Maria Madalena was a fighter, down and dirty, on the street. Any Brazilian ought to understand that.

So the empreiteira business was going good. He was an asset to the company. He and Maria Madalena formed a partnership. Moving on from the really difficult, dirty, and dangerous work to some more respectable factory work, they got the confidence of an electronic parts factory to provide an entire production line. One hundred workers. Dekasegi signed up with him because they believed his pitch, believed him when he said that Brazilians had to support Brazilians, that he was about straight talk, that he wouldn't let his workers sign up without buying health and accident benefits. It was for their own good. Expensive, but he knew what he was talking about. He wasn't going to make promises he couldn't keep. He would keep his if they kept theirs. It was about a man's word and about responsibility, understand?

One day, Maria Madalena was gone. Disappeared. Poof. So was the entire payroll and the benefits fund. Zé Maria ran around in circles like a crazy man. All her clothing was gone, her shoes, her perfumes, her jewelry, her erotic lingerie. Only things left were some photos of her naked body under a pile of panties. My God, what a scandal!

The workers clamored angrily for their money and their rights, which they all knew about because, well, he had told them. They were entitled to severance pay and to a refund on their benefits. Their contract also promised to place them in another job if they lost the current one. The factory closed its doors to them, turned them away, and hired a production line from another empreiteira. Factory representatives said they were sorry, but it wasn't their responsibility. The factory had in fact lost money paid out to the empreiteira for services rendered. One hundred dekasegi were ready to string Zé Maria up and hang him at the door of the factory. Imagine.

Members from the FLU, the Foreign Laborer's Union, showed up to show solidarity for the exploited workers. A coalition of churches and friends of foreigners showed up to offer assistance. Even Maria da Conceição was there, advocating for the victims with her threefold program. Brazilian newspaper journalists covered the events, took depositions and pictures of the angry now-jobless

dekasegi. Zé Maria's photo was everywhere, featured in articles referring to Maria Madalena as his business partner, his girlfriend, his noiva, his consort, with speculations about her whereabouts, probably northern Brazil, possibly the Bahamas.

He had to admit it; he had been duped. What was the poor man going to do? Everyone wanted his neck. He was innocent. Maria Madalena had set him up. He just didn't know it at the time. He thought losing his fingers was payment enough. Yes, he was the President of the company. But it was just a title. Maria Madalena had insisted. She had already gone to jail once for being President, poor thing. Shouldn't someone else take the risk? Now the police were knocking at his door. He was accused of crimes against the Japanese state, serious infractions of the Japanese labor laws. He ran off to the Brazilian Embassy and took sanctuary. He needed some time to think, someone to make his case to in his own language. Shouldn't his own government provide assistance in proving his innocence? This was of international concern. There were larger issues. He was just a convenient scapegoat. There were bigger fish.

Maria da Graça was the liaison for the Brazilian Embassy on matters related to foreign workers in Japan. The jade buttons on her silk jacket were housed in faux gold. She was a bureaucrat who was accustomed to jet-setting around the world, who collected country capitals like free bottles of shampoo in five-star hotels. Her makeup and nails were perfect. Honey, she never had runs in her nylons. She looked at the lump of a man who sat in the leather chair beyond her massive desk and clicked her nails on the dark polished cherrywood. "Mr. Fukuyama, there is no way we can keep you here or hide you. We are guests of the Japanese government and as such are obliged to abide by their laws and regulations."

"But I'm innocent. I didn't steal any money. I'm just being accused because I'm a foreigner. If I were Japanese, no one would bother with me. A Japanese company would find a way to pay up, to hush up everything. Believe me, I know. I've gotten them to pay out money to other dekasegi just to keep things quiet. They don't want to do it this time because I didn't play by their rules, because I'm Brazilian."

"Mr. Fukuyama, as I understand it, one hundred Brazilians have lost their jobs and haven't been paid for an entire month of work."

"I know, I know. I take responsibility for their losses, for Brazilian losses, but I won't be put in a Japanese prison or tried by Japanese laws that only punish a poor dekasegi like me. Don't you see? This is an opportunity to raise some serious issues about the laws

and the empreiteiras. I don't say I was right, but at least I was trying to make things better for others like me. Shouldn't the Brazilian government protect the interests of its citizens abroad? Isn't that the job of the Brazilian Embassy? Isn't that your job?"

Maria da Graça smiled pleasantly. "A lawyer has offered to take your case, and we will accompany the process to see that you are afforded just consideration. I'm sorry, that is the most we are allowed to do."

"But what about international laws, international agreements? Maybe there's some way to bring this out into the open. I'm willing to put my life on the line for this, if it will make a difference." Zé Maria was groping around for a just world, not exactly very Brazilian of him.

"Mr. Fukuyama, do you know the whereabouts of your, ah, partner, Maria Madalena? Perhaps if you were to confess. Japanese law, as you know, is much more lenient where there is demonstrated contrition."

He gripped the cushions of the leather upholstery, clawing it with his absent fingers. He felt his feet sink into the spongy carpets, a springboard ejecting him forward, over the polished cherrywood, unsigned forms, and the desk calendar crammed with scheduled appointments taking flight like a nest of startled chickens.

He wrapped all seven fingers around the bureaucrat's skinny neck. "You're not listening!" he screamed. "I said I'm innocent. I'm so innocent I'm willing to become an international case. I'm so innocent I'm ready to be made an example to the world." He released his fingers, hoping to hear her answer, but her eyes rolled into her head. He grasped chunks of silk and jade buttons housed in faux gold and shook her. "Wake up!  Wake up!" he yelled, to which a dozen Embassy minions responded by tearing into the office and dragging him away. What a scene!

The crime had been committed in the Embassy on Brazilian territory under Brazilian law. And the law was swift and brutal. They shipped him home to Brazil and put him away in prison there. Even Maria da Conceição could do nothing for him, bemoaning the fact to all their activist friends that compared to prisons in Japan, third-world jails were just short of medieval.

Meanwhile, Maria da Graça got reconstituted. No, she didn't die, lucky for Zé Maria. They put her skinny neck in a brace, and she covered it all with color-ful Gucci and Yves Saint Laurent scarves. A classy lady all the way. Now she had her hands full, answering telephone calls. Her voice was a notch lower but still smooth as velvet. She bore her ordeal and never got riled. "Yes, it's a great shame. I understand your difficulty," she commiserated. "I'm told the Brazilian police have some leads, but we shouldn't raise our hopes."

She hung up one phone line and spoke into another. "I'm sorry to keep you waiting. You understand, we are constantly getting calls regarding this situation. If I were you, I would find another job and get on with your life. After all, it's only a month's pay. I don't mean to diminish the extent of your claim, but at least, thank God, it wasn't more. Do you see what I mean?" She continued, "Sankyo Giken? Of course, it's one of the largest empreiteiras, if not the largest, with four branch offices. They must handle 4,000 workers. I'm not in a position to recommend, but of course going with a large company with a large network may be the safest. Again, you understand, this is not advice the Embassy can furnish for you. It's entirely your decision. After all, there are to my knowledge 6,000 empreiteiras in existence."

And to another, "A class action suit against Mr. Fukuyama might be possible, but you would have to make a contractual agreement with the 99 others who lost their paychecks. And you understand that while Mr. Fukuyama is incarcerated in Brazil, there continue to be negotiations regarding the legality of his activities in Japan.

It's very complicated. This is not something the Embassy can accomplish for you. I suggest you consult a lawyer."

And again, "If you paid for health insurance as Mr. Fukuyama insisted, then you are entitled to health services, of course. It's normally about 30,000 yen a year per person. Now that doesn't cover cases of cancer or pregnancy, you understand. No, you weren't cheated at all. It's all very proper, I can assure you. Of course the paperwork is a nuisance, but a necessary nuisance." Smooth as velvet.

Zé Maria should have known, but every once in a while, there's a dekasegi who tries to step off the wheel, who tries to run the program rather than run with it.

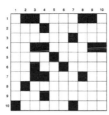

May: Touch Your Heart Circle K

決

T HE FOLLOWING COLLAGE WAS CONSTRUCTED from Japanese English garnered from T-shirts, ads, notebooks, bags, photo albums, towels, food, cars, you name it; along with headlines and ads from the four Brazilian newspapers in Japan: *Folha Mundial, International Press, Jornal Tudo Bem, Nova Visão,* as well as the English publication, *The Japan Times.*

Nikkei mostra penis a japonêsa e vai preso

N.M.O., 27, was arrested on the 27th in Hamamatsu after having exposed his penis to a Japanese woman, M. M., 22. According to police, the Brazilian had also touched the thighs of the victim.

I believe a leaf of grass is no less than the journey work of the stars.

KAREN TEI YAMASHITA

Champion K
International New Sports Association
Exciting Sports Scene.
Complete Power Fulmember
Your energy and health will
be at their this year
Something and Yourself.

Dunga: O samurai da seleção

Captain of the Brazilian World Cup Champion Team currently plays for the Japanese soccer team, Jubilo Iwata. He reveals his opinions about Japanese soccer and his life in Japan in this exclusive interview with *Jornal Tudo Bem.*

Urbane selection for your sweet human living.

Joy Work Corporation Ltd.
Selecting Men, Women, and Couples
AGE: Between 18 and 40 years
TYPE OF SERVICE: Aluminum parts factory
SALARY: Men: 1,300 to 1,500 yen / hr; Women: 900 yen / hr
FURNISHED LODGINGS: 2 persons per apartment
Come work for a solid agency that offers complete assistance.
Call now. Assistance in Portuguese

Dream Time
Happiness is loving someone who loves you.
She is remarkable for her fawn technic.

Polícia resgata reféns da casa do embaixador no Peru

After over four months of crisis, the Peruvian National Police invaded the house of the Japanese ambassador in Lima at 5:23 on April 23 (Japan time) and rescued 72 hostages who were in the hands of the Revolutionary Movement Tupac Amaru (MRTA). According to official reports, all of the guerrillas were killed.

URGENT, MEN WANTED!

LOCALE	Aichi-ken, Toyota-shi, Anjo-shi, and Kariya-shi
TYPE OF SERVICE	Fabrication and mounting of automotive parts
SALARY	Day shift: 11,200 yen / day
	Night shift: 13,510 yen / day
	Overtime: 1,820 yen / hr
	Alternating shifts:
	Day shifts: 8:00-17:00;
	Night shifts: 22:00-7:30
AGE	18 – 40 years
BENEFITS	Health plan, paid vacations, and bonus
FOR INFORMATION, CALL	*World Support*

I never want to lose
the innocence of my heart.
Refreshing times flow gently.
Chirpy

Sakamaki is arrested
Current Nomura chief admits firm erred

Hideo Sakamaki, former president of Nomura Securities Co., was arrested Friday on suspicion of approving illegal payoffs to a "soukai-ya" corporate racketeer to compensate investment losses.

Teddy Market
Old Bear of Project
It's really true when they say
"Many hands make light work."
You'll regret it if you fear it. Think!

Brasileiros processam empreiteiras por salários
Ação foi movida contra a Chubu Seiko, que prejudicou 150 pessoas em Shizuoka.

Brazilians have taken legal action against the hiring agency Chubu Seiko in an attempt to receive unpaid salaries over a period of two months. It's been seven months since the closing of Chubu Seiko. At the time of the agency's closure, many employees were expelled from their lodgings as the agency had failed to pay the rents. The owner, Seishu Hashimoto, has disappeared.

I hope to experience many love affairs.

Investigação: Polícia descobre farsa em assalto de Y3 mi

Brazilian, Roberto Takashi Takanami, 25, was arrested on the 14th, Wednesday, for having invented an assault to justify the disappearance of three million yen . . .

Takanami was an employee of a hiring agency in Toyota and the money would have been used to pay the salary of 20 employees.

Maioria ainda ignora os benefícios dos seguros

Sumiao Kawahara, 48, worked in construction in Ota, Gunma and fell from a height of eight meters, fracturing his tibia and hip. **Elza Koga,** 42, of Sakai, Gunma, fractured her foot under a forklift. **Nelson Nakata,** 32, of Kani, Gifu, lost his index finger two years ago. **Claudio Ogata,** 21, of Anjo, Aichi, lost his finger. **George Shinohara,** 12, of Hamamatsu had his left foot amputated and part of the right leg bone due to cancer.

---

america
Since 1982
original range of casual wear from California
Beverly Hills Polo Club

Brasileiros ficam revoltados com declaração de político

Japanese Representative, Juichiro Yamagawa, of the Shinseikai Party of Hamamatsu, angered the community in Japan when he stated that Brazilians dissatisfied with the health insurance system should return to their home country.

KAREN TEI YAMASHITA

Public announcement reported in stores:

Attention shoppers and clerks! Foreigners have entered the premises. Shoppers, please take care to secure your personal belongings. Clerks, please watch for possible theft of merchandise.

Joky gal
Your heart will dance to
Sincerity American style

For sophisticate woman
I'm particular about fashion
and personal things.
And that's what I'd like to share with you.

DESTAQUE: **Vanessa**

NAME: **Vanessa Cristina Iaketa, 19, from Santos-SP.** She's been in Japan three years and lives in Oizumi, Gunma.

JAPAN: "It's a good place to live as long as you have family."

PREFERRED FOOD: "Anything as long as it's seafood."

SPORT: "Ice Skating"

QUALITY: "Honesty"

DEFECT: "I'm too possessive."

SEX: "Natural, as long as it's with love."

LOVE: "Very difficult to explain."

MESSAGE: "Everyone who comes to Japan should have well-defined objectives in order not to lose your way."

Acidente mata brasileiro; japonêsa assume a culpa

Claudio Tsutomo Utsunomiya, 21, died in a collision with another car in Nagano. The driver of the oncoming car had fallen asleep.

Your trip with nature
will always be a pleasant
environmental adventure.

KDD investe Y300 mi no sistema callback

The Kokusai Denshin Denwa (KDD), the Japanese international telephone company, is investing 300 million yen in Forval International Telecommunications (FIT), a leading company in the international system of callback, with its headquarters in Tokyo.

STAY BACK
200 FT

Ajudar imigrante ilegal leva a prisão

Helping illegal immigrants may result in a prison sentence of five years and a fine of three million yen. The Diet Judicial Committee approved unanimously the new immigration law to tighten control of the entry of illegal foreigners in Japan.

Please tempting the taste of Hide beef

Looks good. Tastes good, too. Right?
Did you know I am a famous cook in Japan?
I have my own restaurant!

Plaspa Meat Shop & Restaurant

Karaoke in Portuguese!!

ALL YOU CAN EAT BUFFET SATURDAYS & SUNDAYS!!

1,000 YEN — SUPER PROMOTIONS!!

Ribs	480 yen / kg
Steaks	780 yen / kg
Pork Sausages	850 yen / kg
Pig's feet / Tail / Ear	600 yen / kg
Fish (Pintado)	2000 yen / kg
Fish (Piranha)	1100 yen / kg

Delivery direct to your home anywhere in Japan!

MINISTOP FF = FAST FOOD ... WHAT'S?
*Flash Food * Formal Food*
*Famous Food * Fairyfood * Fight Food*
*Floral Food * Feeling Food*
*Flying Food * Fever Food*
*Faithful Food * Fire Food*
Fall in Love Food

Criatividade:

Harumaki with hearts of palm and mochi in a green sauce are dishes created by Sadako Cida Doi, chef, who has won the admiration of the Japanese.

ABERTA NOVA LANCHONETE

Twelve kinds of pastel, seven varieties of pizza, twelve different sandwiches, and thirteen dishes of canapés in an ambiance of a typical Brazilian bar are the delicacies of the newly opened K-Pastel, in Hamamatsu, in the prefecture of Shizuoka.

> *Waffle Furato Shitsu*
> *Here is a small white flying*
> *And there, a honeybee's popped out.*
> *Some flowers have just begun to come out, here and there.*
> *It's about time for me to burst into bloom, now!*

Barbie paralítica não pega no Brasil (Paralytic Barbie Doll doesn't make it in Brazil) Nova boneca foi lançada nos Estados Unidos e já vende mais que a "normal."

Pickachu is your friend

Casal real fala da visita ao Brasil

During an interview, the Emperor and Empress remember friends and dekasegi, to whom they send their good wishes. The Emperor stated, "I will be very happy if this (dekasegi phenomenon) results in opportunities for more interchange between the people of our countries. I hope that their stay in Japan will be fruitful and that they can make good friends here before they return to their country."

> *Petite note*
> *Let simple and old fashioned myself*
> *stay with you, while ordinary things*
> *have been disappearing in the world.*

Brasileiro mata família e tenta suicídio

The wife of Brazilian, Alberto Abe, 36, was killed by knifing on Thursday night, 15th, in Inuyama, prefecture of Aichi. It is suspected that he also killed his two daughters, one five-year-old and the other seven months, incinerating the bodies in the smelting ovens where he works. Abe attempted suicide, but was saved. The motives that led the Brazilian to commit the crime are unknown, but are perhaps related to depression provoked by a health problem.

> *Both a bird in the sky and*
> *we are the same creature.*
> *They tell us the truth that*
> *if you want to take the*
> *lively pictures,*
> *you have to feel the breath of them.*

Note Avenue

Times simply too very important to afford to be forgotten are the true substance of our memories.

Homi Danchi corre risco de virar cenário de batalha

A series of incidents (vandalism, noise from motorcycles at midnight, and loud music) have disturbed the routine of the condominium complex of Homi Danchi, housing 2,500 Brazilians in Toyota. The Homeowners Association inscribed a series of regulations on a large sign with a translation in Portuguese. Among the rules are the prohibitions of throwing trash from the windows and of having barbecues. After various frustrated attempts to live better with the strangers, the Association asked the police and public entities for a larger participation in the solution to their problems.

Dream Collection
So many wonderful
dreams, wherever we go!
Dream collectors, all:
let's make every dream our own!

Jovens estariam consumindo droga em Hamamatsu — Game Center

According to a central police bulletin dated May 22 in Hamamatsu, an 18-year-old Brazilian was arrested for drugs on May 7 at 8:13 P.M.

Imóveis no Brasil — Your Real Estate in Brazil
Boa oportunidade para compra de populares está no Grande ABC

Arco-Íris Residential Condominium is located in the center of São Bernardo do Campo, with 296 apartments, a useful area of 43 square meters, and a leisure area of 1,200 square meters.

Witness the sky above is blue and infinite the great sun is white and scorching the seagulls are coolly sailing.

Apenas 31% dos alunos estrangeiros conhecem o idioma japonês para entrar no colegial

Around half of the foreign junior high students in Japanese schools wish to enter high school, but only 31% of them are proficient enough in the Japanese language necessary to accompany classes, a study by the Tokyo Gakugei University revealed last month.

Individuality opens up an age
actual feeling
Unintentionally with individuality
and nonchalantly with sensibility
Toroppa designed by LeCien

Brasileiro preso denuncia 2 alunos por consumir droga
15-year-old students confess using crack in Hamamatsu.

Doraemon is the cat type robot.

All children grows up little by little and
Childhood turns into only a memory.
The smile is full of the urge to do mischief.

Faleceu difusor da pedagogia dos oprimidos
Brazil lost one of its great activists in education. Paulo Freire, 75 years, teacher and writer, father of five children, died on May 2 in Albert Einstein Hospital, from heart problems.

When you put your body in the Mother Nature. You sure feel the greatness of the god creation it embraces you tenderly and wash your agony you picked up in your life off the grand view and the connoted wisdom.

—Alpine Equipment Baboleta, Croster Dragon

I'm Nudy. Who are you?
Hair Water Milk

> **Polícia busca esfaqueador que**
> **matou casal brasileiro**
>
> **Woman found dead in suitcase with**
> **head and hands exposed.**
>
> The Brazilian couple, Carlos Alberto Osako, 30, and Masayo Fujiharu, 30, were found dead by knifing on Saturday, April 26, in Fukui. The body of the man was rolled up in a blanket and was discovered by a woman walking on route 364, next to a tunnel in Maruoka-cho.

A photograph can
run our imaginary writing brush,
give us a free emotion.
The one who heartily releases numerous shutters
of the subjects with rising emotion,
he will be able to open a happy exhibition.

"Crime da mala" apavora brasileiros
Mystery: police discover blood in the house
and interrogate hiring agencies
Signs of blood found in the interior of the duplex where the couple, Carlos Alberto Oseko and Masayo Fujiharu (left, in a photo provided by the family) . . .

BRASILEIROS DESAPARECIDOS
BRAZILIANS MISSING

NAME: **Antonio Hideaki Araki**
AGE: 52 years
LAST ADDRESS: Ibaraki-ken, Ishioka-shi
CONTACT IN BRAZIL: Lourdes

NAME: **Roberto Hitoshi Toge**
AGE: 37 years
LAST ADDRESS: Kanagawa-ken, Yokosuka-shi
CONTACT IN BRAZIL: Neusa

NAME: **Alex Morais Tomioka**
AGE: 17 years
CONTACT IN JAPAN: Loja Nadaya (Koorien Station) Neyagawa-shi, Mr. Akita

Peruvian President Alberto Fujimori denies being born in Japan

Documentation and a photograph of Alberto Fujimori as a child have been alleged to prove that Fujimori was in fact born in Japan and, therefore, by constitutional law ineligible to be President of Peru.

Recado

"To my dear wife Helena, I wish you a happy birthday. And that God gives you health and many years of life. These are the hopes of your husband who loves you very much."

—From Iochio Ito, Sukagawa, Fukushima

I love every bone in your body including my own.

Circling Katakana

生

JAPANESE, CERTAINLY NOT UNLIKE ENGLISH, IS A KIND OF pidgin language, borrowing broadly—its writing system from China and, lately, the words that name its technological and cosmopolitan society from America. The writing system encompasses three character systems: kanji, hiragana, and katakana. Kanji, of which you require the knowledge of 2,000 to be functionally literate, is the system of character signs that Japan adopted from China. Hiragana is a phonetic system of about 51 sounds and the writing system indigenous to Japan. Those of us who don't want to memorize 2,000 kanji always wonder why hiragana wasn't good enough for the Japanese. After all, Murasaki Shikibu wrote what's considered perhaps the world's first novel, *Genji Monogatari (The Tale of Genji),* entirely in hiragana. One imagines that novels were considered frivolous; in the 10th century, the

神話

KAREN TEI YAMASHITA

"real" thinking was done by men and in Chinese characters. The hierarchy in the *authority* of writing is of course nothing new.

Katakana is a blocky looking version of hiragana. The difference between katakana and hiragana is like the difference between block printing and script or maybe Courier and Chancery fonts. Katakana was created as a phonetic guide for chanting Buddhist sutras and later for writing poetry. Coming into use around the 8th century, katakana probably predates hiragana which later became a kind of cursive form. Despite its noble past, katakana is today used mostly to write foreign words and maybe the sounds of animals and the like. In order to read Japanese, you need to learn all three writing systems, but generally children and foreigners new to the language begin with katakana.

Years ago, as a high school student, I received a set of Japanese language records, a part of a new aural learning system. My nisei parents, who grew up hearing the language, scoffed at the speaker who made the recordings. Hambaga, she said and repeated. Kohi, she said. It was katakana, and it was English. Well, sort of. Just because you can read katakana and it's likely to be an English word, doesn't necessarily mean you can understand it. This isn't just true for us American gaijin who stare at signs and mouth the sounds until we

フジカラーだから、パレットプラザのプリントだから、さらにいい色。

get an inkling of the meaning. It's also true for the Japanese who require katakana dictionaries to decipher these words. Pasokon for example. It means personal computer. Or kon-bini; that means convenience store. How  about borantia? It means volunteer. Hambaga was easy. Or what about sekuhara? Now that word has a kanji invented for it, and it means sexual harassment. After you get the hang of katakana, you can understand why cars are named Celica, Accord, Camry, or Corolla. Furthermore, as I write these car names, the spell check in Microsoft Word doesn't even blink an eye. Well, it doesn't like Camry . . .

Nowadays you can buy a katakana dictionary to keep up with all the new words invading the language. Looking through it, there isn't much you can't say in katakana. A-teifisharu raifu: artificial life. Konshu-marisumu: consumerism. To-ku sho: talk show. Faji-kon-pyu-ta: fuzzy computer. Poa howaito: poor white. Maruchipa-pasu porishi: multipurpose policy. Reiba-inten-shibu: labor intensive. Wakki: wacky. I figure that if we can get katakana to sign on to English verbs, I can just about write a novel in it. *Za Teiru obu Genji.*

For years now, the Japanese have been stuffing American words into katakana. This is really disconcerting for other foreigners who are expected to know English too. A Brazilian friend and I both approached the McDonald's counter to make our orders. My friend is far more fluent in Japanese than I am, but she puzzled over the clerk's question: dorinku? I answered Koka-Kora, but she stood there confused. If she heard the word drinque, to Brazilians it means an alcoholic mixed drink. Since when had McDonald's started serving alcohol? Then of course, when did drinque become a Portuguese word?

Lately since my writing has been translated to Japanese, I've noticed that my name as the author is always written in katakana. Well, it's the only part of the translation I can actually read anyway. So it hurts me to see that my last name Yamashita is not written in kanji. It's after all an easy set of kanji: yama and shita (mountain and under). And my middle name Tei, named after my Meiji Japanese grandmother, is also not written in hiragana. Ka-ren, okay. That's the katakana in me. I like the hybridity of my name, the pidginess of it, but it's all been reduced to that block lettering, a phonetic approximation that designates my foreignness, facilitates my illiteracy, sends a  textual signal to the reader. Since I cannot read the translation of my work, I don't know how much of it, other than my name, is apportioned to katakana, but it's a curious thought; maybe I am writing in katakana.

保証は付いていますか。

54

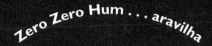

Zero Zero Hum . . . aravilha

業

Alô, Maria Maravilha às suas ordens. Pois não, eu estou reconhecendo sua voz. Quem? Pois é claro. Eu sempre me lembro da voz de um homem bonitão. Tudo bem se você nunca ligou antes. Sempre tem uma primeira vez, não é mesmo? Para falar a verdade, tudo não passa de fingimento. Não dá em nada se você não tiver uma boa imaginação. Espere só um pouquinho. Vou passar para meu quarto. Okay?

Estar hantai /
Estar de cabeça prá baixo

Alice, tem um cara na outra linha mas, ele pode esperar. Como eu tava dizendo, eu estava pulando no mar como uma criança livre sem preocupações, quando de repente caí num buraco, um rodamoinho, afundando como um pedaço de merda. Não deu tempo de reagir. Pensei que fosse meu fim. Você tá rindo? Juro por Deus que é verdade. Espera um minutinho.

Maria Madalena Oliveira Shinbashi, dançarina artística, 28, original de São Paulo, foi vista pela última vez no Saci Pererê em Shinjuku. Um mandato de prisão foi expedido. Qualquer informação sobre seu paradeiro deve ser dirigida ao departamento de polícia de Tokyo.

Dar um sampo / Dar uma andada

Vou te dizer uma coisa menina, juro que é a pura verdade mesmo que ninguém acredite em mim. Era uma noite linda em maio. Agora eu posso ver, como se fosse ontem: uma lua cheia, linda, dançando no mar, pulando as ondas como se fosse um coelho. E eu, como uma boba, correndo atrás dela. Não, não, Alice, naquela época eu era virgenzinha da silva. Okay, talvez eu tivesse com um pouco de maconha na cabeça. Isso era uma alegria inocente. Espere um pouco aí. O outro telefone está tocando. Deixa eu ver quem é, só um minutinho.

KAREN TEI YAMASHITA

Maria Madalena. Yoshiwara Shimbashi, prostituta, 32, natural de Curitiba, foi vista pela última vez no Paraíso Latino em Kawasaki, com o baterista Alexandre Ozaki. Ao ser interrogado pelos investigadores, Ozaki declarou que Shinbashi não parecia ter nenhum plano de imediato. Ele estranhou seu desaparecimento. É atribuído a Shinbashi o extravio de fundos a serem pagos aos empregados sob contrato através da agência de recursos humanos Tudo Daijobi, de sua propriedade, no valor de 5.5 milhões de yens.

Ser mattaku japonês / gaijin / Ser puramente japonês / estrangeiro

Alô. Está melhor assim. Agora estou no meu quarto. Aqui podemos falar com mais intimidade. Vamos ver.... Estávamos falando de sua imaginação. Você pode usar sua imaginação como quiser. Meu cabelo, por exemplo. Que cor de cabelo você gosta? Acertou em cheio. Sou loirinha da cabeça aos pés.

Você não acredita? A foto do jornal? Acho que não é a minha foto. Para te dizer a verdade eles colocam a foto que querem. Bem, deveriam usar a foto de uma loira. Os japoneses adoram loiras. Você não é japonês? Pois é claro que não é. Você é brasileiro. De onde? Mato Grosso do Sul? Nossa, que longe! Não conheço nada daquele lado mas dizem que é muito bonito. Quero que você me conte tudo de lá mas primeiro deixa eu pegar uma cerveja. Tudo bem. Volto num minutinho.

Magdalena Shinbashi do Rio de Janeiro e Tokyo era conhecida por ser uma ex-atriz e hostess em Shinjuku. Começou sua agencia de contratos de emprego e ficou famosa por ter sido a primeira e única empregadora a ser presa devido às suas atividades.

Cair do tatami / Cair da cama

Alice, é só um garotão na outra linha. Sinto uma peninha dele. Longe da mamãe. Vou dar um bom trato nele. É assim que eu sou. Me apaixono por todos meus clientes. Voltando à nossa conversa, caí no centro da terra, escor- regando dentro de uma onda mas devo ter tido um choque. Talvez eu tenha dormido. Perdi completamente o senso de tempo. Pois é claro que eu não estou mentindo.

お言づけお願い出来ますか。

Um dia estava em casa , no outro acordei aqui. Pode acreditar. A terceira linha tá tocando. Espere um minutinho.

Moshi moshi. Páginas Verde-Amarelas! A única lista telefônica no Japão publicada por brasileiros. Em que posso ser útil? Ah Carlinhos, você é justamente a pessoa com quem eu queria conversar. Bem, como você já sabe, esse ano estamos querendo incrementar as Páginas. Além das ofertas de novos empregos aqui no Japão, queremos oferecer o melhor serviço, entendeu? Por exemplo, nossos cupons de desconto poderão ser utilizados. Acho que seria uma ótima idéia se você desse descontos para os clientes que têm assinatura do seu serviço telefônico. Você já tem um quarto de página em anúncios, que tal investir um pouco mais em postais inseridos nos anúncios? Eu posso te mandar um exemplo por fax. Carlinhos, você vai ter que me desculpar. É que tem um outro cliente me esperando na outra linha. Para dizer a verdade é seu concorrente, IDC (International Digital Communications). Mas não se preocupe. Volto já, mas tenho quase certeza que ele vai querer a página inteira de anúncios. Até posso estar enganada mas, acho que não.

Maria Maravilha Shinbashi, residente de Roppongi, desapareceu e é acusada de sumir com fundos destinados ao pagamento dos empregados. Seu sócio, Zé Maria Fukuyama, nega ser seu cúmplice no tocante ao fundo desviado, na importância de 55 milhões de yens. Ele se mostrou surpreso quando sua sócia Shinbashi desapareceu repentinamente.

Fazer kampai / Fazer um brinde

Oi benzinho, pegou sua cerveja gelada? Está confortável? Onde é mesmo que estávamos? Mato Grosso do Sul? Você sabia que eu sou do Rio? Faz tanto tempo que estou longe de casa. . . . Há quanto tempo você está aqui? Só 2 anos? Então espera até quando você estiver aqui 7 anos como eu. Cê nunca vai se acostu-

No mês dos namorados, faça o coração do seu amor bater mais forte!

mar. Cê veio sozinho? E aquela namorada que você deixou lá? Ah não, me conta tudinho. Que triste! Pois é claro que ela ainda te ama. Para sempre, tenho certeza. E sua mãe? Pois é claro que não pode dizer prá ela que isso aqui é uma droga mas, de todo jeito ela é sua mãe. Cê vai voltar logo com certeza. É uma questão de tempo. Aposto que cê vai ver sua mãe com vida de novo. Pode chorar, bem. Chora mesmo. Põe tudo para fora. Cê tá me fazendo chorar também. Espere aí, eu vou buscar um lenço.

Maria Madalena Shinbashi está provavelmente nas Bahamas.

Ser mulher do obento /
Ser a mulher que fornece marmita

Alice, você ainda está esperando? Meu cliente está morrendo de chorar. Explico mais tarde mas nesse compasso não vou conseguir contar nada para você. O que cê tá fazendo? Fritando? Bife à milanesa? Quantos? Cem? Quem diria, hein, que você ia virar mulher do obento? Não se esqueça que fui eu que arrumei seu primeiro emprego. Bem, continue cozinhando. Eu já volto.

Carlos, gomen,ne. A competição tá danada, hein? Como eu estava dizendo, meia página para IDC. Pelo amor de Deus! Por que você não compra uma página inteira ou até duas. Soube que os brasileiros gastam 4 bilhões de yens por ano em chamadas telefônicas internacionais. Além do que, a KDD é a maior companhia telefônica do Japão. Dizem que tem 200 mil milhas de cabos. É verdade? Nossa Páginas vão aparecer em todas bancas de jornal por onde os brasileiros passam. E mais ainda, a Varig está pensando em dar as Páginas de brinde para os passageiros. Os dekasseguis vão desembarcar com ela. Vocês têm um negócio de telefonia e nós temos a lista

57

O que mais você gostaria? Mais um momento, por favor. O outro telefone está tocando. Tá vendo? Está todo mundo brigando para anunciar conosco.

Maria Magdalena Shinbashi foi vista na Bahia.

Meu beeem, meu beeem. Você está bem ? Não se envergonhe. É para isso que estou aqui. Você sente minha voz no seu ouvidinho? Ajuda? Meus lábios estão tão perto do seu ouvido. Se eu esticar minha língua eu posso sentir o sal bem na pontinha. Isso. Sinto você através do telefone. Me diga o que sente. Meesmo? Bem então vou ter que me trocar. Você sabe que acabei de chegar em casa. Estou com esses jeans super apertados. Espera um pouquinho para eu tirar minha calça? Espere por mim, amorzinho.

Ser deka / Ser um dekassegui

Carlinhos, decidiu? Enquanto você está decidindo, já vendi mais 2 anúncios. Deixe te contar uma coisa. O que você me paga só cobre o custo. Esse é um trabalho que faço por amor. Não ganho um centavo. O que falta ao dekassegui é informação. Ele é um animal completamente sem conhecimento sobre o Japão, da língua, dos costumes, conexões . . . Pobrezinhos. Você acha que o Consulado ajuda em alguma coisa? Quase nada. Precisamos melhorar essa situação. Uns brasileiros me

pessoalmente que as *Páginas Verde-Amarelas!* são a publicação mais útil que eles encontraram. E não é um ou dois, não mas um monte deles. Está todo mundo esperando a próxima edição. A última vez publicamos 25 mil e, em uma semana, vendemos tudo. Tivemos que imprimir mais 10 mil e ainda assim não foi suficiente. Se você investir um pouco mais talvez possamos fazer um pouco mais. Espere um minutinho na linha.

Maria Madalena foi vista em Belém.

Alice, como está a comida? E o arroz? Está pronto? Tô cuma fome! E seus planos para abrir um internet café? Que nome você tá pensando em dar? Cafénette? Os caras vão para comer, beber e ficar um tempinho na internet. Bem, você já tem a cozinha. O que você precisa é pôr mais mesas. Seu investimento maior será em computadores mas eu sei que você tem o dinheiro. Espere um pouquinho na linha.

Voltei queridinho. Desculpe por te deixar esperando. Vesti uma roupa rosa transparente. Use sua imaginação. E um perfume especial, bem afrodisíaco, sabe como é? Me deixa louca de desejo. Também pus um baton bem vermelho. Meus lábios estão em fogo. Você não parece entusiasmado. Ainda tá triste, pensando na mamãe? Não fique bravo, querido. Eu sei que você

好評発売中

paga por minuto mas, mesmo assim não precisa ser grosso. A mulher precisa se preparar, você não sabe disso? Comigo não é só tirar, enfiar, gozar e pronto. Há um ritual envolvendo isso. Você precisa aprender a ter modos, meu bem. Olha, quando estiver pronto, me ligue. Estarei aqui. Tchau.

Dizem que Maria Madalena Shinbashi está em Bali.

Wakatar / Compreender

Okay Carlinhos, vou aceitar seu pedido. Negócio fechado. Você vai ter várias páginas com postais inseridos para KDD. Você vai ver quantas assinaturas novas vai conseguir através de nossas páginas. Não. Não. Chega de discussões

sobre isso. Você já me convenceu. Eu sei como as coisas ficaram difíceis nesse negócio de chamadas telefônicas. Nós já conseguimos 10 anúncios para companhias de retorno de chamadas telefônicas. Pense nisso! As chamadas de retorno custam metade do preço de KDD! Eu estou te ajudando, puxa vida! Mando seu contrato amanhã. Deixa comigo. Você está fazendo pelo negócio mas também para servir a comunidade. Estou cansada de tratar os brasileiros no Japão como se fossem incapazes. O maior problema deles é a língua e estas páginas se traduzem em sobrevivência básica. Tchau, Carlinhos. Aguarde meu fax.

KAREN TEI YAMASHITA

Ela escondeu o dinheiro numa conta bancária em Singapura.

Sair do teiji / Sair da rotina

Alice, finalmente, por um momento, estou livre dos negócios. Onde mesmo que eu estava? Caindo num buraco e depois desmaiando, certo? Então, quando finalmente abri os olhos, lá estava eu numa cama de botões de flores de cereja, rodeada por um perfume doce, naquela cama tão macia, botões caindo por todo lado. Pensei que tivesse morrido mas, quando eu olhei bem à minha volta eu estava na realidade sob os refletores de luzes e câmeras. Tinha um ventilador assoprando pétalas por toda parte e um

じゃ、また電話します。

diretor velho, de boné, gritando o que se deveria fazer. E se não bastasse, eu estava nua. Devo ter perdido meu bikini na queda. Foi horrível! Meu cabelo estava grudado que nem alga marinha, e meus peitos e bumbum melados com areia e pedaços de conchas marinhas. Não era sonho. De jeito nenhum. Eu estava tão acordada como agora. Juro. Você acha que eu sou esquizofrênica ou coisa parecida? Ah, de novo! Outra chamada.

Ser karaoqueiro / Ser cantor de karaokê

Moshi moshi. *Páginas Verde-Amarelas!* Aqui, para ajudar os brasileiros da melhor maneira possível. Como posso lhe ser útil? Consideramos a Páginas um serviço para a comunidade. Vamos publicar todos os números de negócios brasileiros, sem dúvidas. Salões de beleza, escolas, bares, exportação / importação, empreiteiras, agências de viagem, carne pelo correio, serviços de escort. Publicamos tudo. Qual seu tipo de serviço? Karaoqueiro?

Pois é claro que queremos incluir artistas como você. Por que não? Músicos, capoeiristas, bateiristas, cantores. Agora, se você estiver interessado em outro anúncio além do seu número de telefone, tem um pequeno acréscimo. Mas se puder investir um pouco mais será mais vantajoso para você e, nos ajudaria muito nos custos da publicação. Nós brasileiros precisamos de uma rede de comunicação. Uma vez que você é parte dessa rede, vai encontrar maiores possibilidades de uma melhora de vida aqui. Uma pessoa como você com um talento especial, merece uma chance melhor. Que tal um anúncio de 1/8 de página, com sua foto? Maravilha. Você vai ver. Nada se ganha sem um pouco de investimento. Mando um contrato por correio, okay?

Fontes dizem que ela depositou o dinheiro secretamente numa conta bancária em Bangkok.

Estar tudo barabara / Estar tudo bagunçado
Alice, já vendi várias páginas de anúncios hoje. Mas voltando à minha estória. Eu estava nuazinha, correndo

prá lá e prá cá. Sem escapatória. O cameraman correndo atrás de mim. O filme ganhou prêmios em Cannes. Eu impressionei bem, naturalmente. Foi assim que cheguei ao Japão. Um acidente completo, sem documentos, nem mesmo um trapo para me cobrir. Que vergonha! Eu choro só de lembrar. Talvez haja outros que chegaram como eu mas não conheço ninguém. Você e os outros chegaram normalmente, pela Varig, Vasp, KAL e JAL. Mesmo assim, vocês todos chegam nus também. Nus metaforicamente, pois é claro. No meu caso está tudo registrado em filme. Aí vem outro cliente.

Investigadores estão analisando relatórios em que ela depositou fundos numa conta bancária em Vancouver.

Gambatear / Persistir
Alô? Quem é? Sérgio? Está difícil para te escutar, querido. Onde você está? Numa estação de trem? Num orelhão? É, aqui é Maria Maravilha. Pois é claro que é meu nome de verdade. Não, não dá prá me encontrar com você. Você está com o pau duro? Mesmo? Fala mais disso. Onde você disse que está? Impossível. Eu estou em Tokyo. Por que não me liga de novo de algum outro lugar, onde vamos dizer assim, onde eu possa aliviar sua tensão? Você mora com mais 6 caras? Que merda, hein! Se você vier prá Tokyo? Oh não. Você não me acharia aqui. Nem se preocupe amorzinho. Oh, Oh, seu cartão telefônico está acabando . . .

Alice, o feijão tá pronto? Tô morrendo de vontade de comer feijão. Quem podia imaginar que você ficaria tão prendada, hein? Tá bem que você era mãe com filhos mas, aposto que você não cozinhava naquela época—ou era sua mãe ou a empregada. Você sempre fala de sua

じゃ、また電話します。

vinda prá cá como o começo de uma nova vida. Liberdade é a palavra que você usa. Já entendi. Tudo bem que seu ex-marido no Brasil era um bebum. É meu telefone rosa de novo. Geralmente só toca nos fins de semana. É melhor eu não reclamar; ele paga minhas contas.

Relatórios afirmam que ela tem uma conta bancária em Porto Príncipe.

Estar genqui / Estar bem

Alô? Decidiu ligar de novo? Eu brava? Bem, um pouquinho. Você briga com sua namorada? Você começa a briga ou é ela? Quem é ciumento? É ela? Bem, talvez ela tenha motivo para ser ciumenta. Você liga sempre prá ela? Toda semana? Você não tem me ligado toda semana? Não é você? Eu jurava que era. Você e sua namorada trepam por telefone? Bem vocês deveriam, então. Já entendi. Bem, pelo menos você tem algo para se entusiasmar. Concordo 100%. Falar no telefone não prejudica ninguém. Sexo seguro. Eu não faria isso de outra maneira. Os ricos e famosos fazem isso o tempo todo. Presidente Clinton,

Diana . . . Lógico, me liga a qualquer hora. Maria Maravilha está sempre à sua disposição.

Alice, por que você não põe um anúncio nas *Páginas?* Eu te dou um desconto. Que tal o nome de Alice's Cafénette. *Tome uma cerveja com um pastel enquanto você surfa a net.* Talvez a gente possa colocar as Páginas on-line num website. Ouvi falar que a gente pode fazer uma fortuna em anúncios. Outra chamada. Bem, eu não deveria reclamar, mas bem que o dinheiro podia ser melhor.

Moshi moshi. *Páginas Verde-Amarelas!* Apresentando os brasileiros para a rede de comunicações japonesa. Com quem gostaria de falar? Ana? Você não está mais trabalhando para o *Jornal Tudo Bem?* Aposto que você está no *International Press,* então. Não? Para a *Folha Mundial?* Quando? Bem, tenho uma proposta. Você compra um anúncio para seu jornal nas Páginas e eu compro um anúncio do seu. Negócio fechado. Assim ajudamos a  *Folha* e você ajuda as *Páginas.* Anúncios por anúncios. Pronto. Ana, você deve conhecer essas revistas novas como *Made in Japão* e *Aqui Japão.* Que tal a TV a cabo? Estou tentando convencê-los de anunciar conosco. Pode me dar seus contatos? Ótimo. Fico te devendo essa. Tchau.

KAREN TEI YAMASHITA

Ela foi vista na companhia de pessoas desagradáveis.

Falar de keitai / Falar no celular

Quem está falando? Marcelo? Você é um cara muito antipático! Onde você está? Eu estou escutando barulho de máquinas. É uma fábrica, não é? Você está na hora do café? Você não pode me xingar por estar perturbando. Quem colou minha foto naquele máquina? Você poderia perder um dedo?

Minha culpa? Mas você não perdeu nem um dedo ou seu pau por conta daquilo. Oh benzinho, essa maquinaria pesada me dá tesão também. Vamos resolver isso de uma vez por todas. Você está no celular? Então encontre um lugar e me ligue de novo.

Alice, eu sei que você não acredita na minha estória mas não tem nenhuma explicação. Eu não perdi a memória. Cheguei sem visto e sem passaporte, sem nenhum tipo de informação. Vida nova, meu bem! Comecei do zero. Tive que fazer tudo sozinha. Aprendi a língua sozinha. Tem uns brasileiros que estão aqui há 7 anos e não sabem falar nada além de pedir para ir ao banheiro. Eles chegam aqui achando que a vida deve algo a eles. Ai, ai, ai, mais um . . .

Marcelo? Onde você tá? Num banheiro? É extremamente deprimente, mas por você, estou aí também. Eu vou te chupar a seco e você não pode me culpar pelo que acontecer. Promete? Não, você tem que prometer. Ok, você está escutando? Abriu o zíper? *Alô? Alô?*

Alice, caiu a linha. Acho que meu cliente derrubou o celular na privada. Vou atender outra chamada para as Páginas. Pare de rir.

Ela foi vista em companhia de membros de um cartel de drogas colombiano.

Shigotar / trabalhar

Moshi, moshi. *Páginas Verde-Amarelas!* Trabalhando para ajudar os brasileiros a realizarem seus sonhos. Como posso ajudá-lo? Nossa publicação está programada para agosto. Pois é claro que gostaríamos de coincidir a data de publicação com os festivais de agosto para chamar a atenção da comunidade. Por exemplo, estaremos no Samba Matsuri em Oizumi. Uma excelente oportunidade para promover as *Páginas*. Tem mais de 300 negócios de brasileiros funcionando hoje em dia no Japão. E o número aumenta todo dia. As *Páginas* vão triplicar em tamanho. Se deixarmos só 100 cópias da *Páginas* em cada loja, já temos 30 mil

Páginas para fornecer. Pense nisso! As *Páginas* de fato representam a superfície de uma enorme rede de negócios brasileiros no Japão. Agora sem dúvida, você como uma empreiteira tem interesse em estar ligado a esse imenso recurso. O primeiro interesse de qualquer dekassegui é sempre encontrar trabalho. Meia página? Ótimo. Eu te envio nosso contrato por fax. Muito simples, sem complicação. Obrigada por nos ter procurado.

Estar de yakin / Estar de plantão noturno

Alice, desde que cheguei aqui, tenho tido uma educação especial. Meu primeiro emprego foi como hostess num bar de karaoke de 1ª classe em Roppongi. Eles ofereciam sake com pedacinhos de papel de ouro boiando na bebida. Além de ouro, sabe Deus que outras substâncias eles manuseavam. Eu tentava não me meter em encrenca. Eu tinha que ser mais esperta do que eles imaginavam, tinha que aprender a ficar acordada. Eu não ia cair em outro buraco. Quem é que sabe aonde eu iria acabar? Você pensa que pode ficar acordada só por um certo tempo mas, Tokyo deixa você acordada por mais tempo. Você pode ficar acordada para sempre, num sonho sem fim. Espere um pouco na linha.

Alô? É mesmo? Do jeito que você está falando parece que bebeu a garrafa inteira. Pois é claro que não. Eu mesma tou tomando uma cerveja agora. Relaxe. O Japão é muito estressante! Eu sei o que você quer dizer. Você não sente saudades de simples- *mente ficar num bar de esquina, comendo batatinha frita e azeitona, se esquentando no sol da tarde sem ter que fazer nada? Eu entendo o que você quer dizer. Eu sempre encontrava meu pai à tarde no bar da esquina jogando carta e dadinho. Me conta sua diversão preferida. Me conta. Alô? Ah ...*

Ela foi vista com traficantes de drogas bolivianos.

Tsukaretar / Ficar cansado(a)

Alice, meu cliente dormiu. Ele paga por minuto mas está dormindo feito um bobo. Ele trabalha extra só prá me ligar no seu tempo livre. Ele poderia pachinkar[1] mas, prefere me telefonar. O resto do dinheiro ele manda para a mãe dele em Goiânia. Gritar para ele acordar? Eu não. Deixe ele em paz.

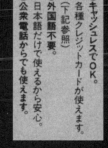

Mas como eu estava dizendo, o mundo sob as ruas de Tokyo está sempre ligado, oxigênio bombado para dentro e o monóxido de carbono para fora. As entranhas de Tokyo são um Godzilla retorcido respirando por você. Nesse submundo aprendi a viver do jeito japonês. Alguém já te falou de honne/tatemae? É o que está dentro e o que está fora. O brasileiro nunca aprende isso mas é essencial para a vida aqui. Ele acha que o que vê é o que é a realidade mas o japonês nunca vê nada desse

---

[1] logar pachinko, um jogo, pinball game

jeito. Para o japonês, tudo pode ser outra coisa. Tudo pode mudar. Tudo tem um interior verdadeiro e uma casca que o cobre. Até a frente de algo pode ser questionada. Eu tenho um telefone azul, por exemplo, mas isso nunca estará claro para um japonês. Ele vai dizer que talvez seja azul. Poderia ser azul? Possivelmente é azul. É realmente azul? O que é o azul? Devemos concordar que é azul? O brasileiro que só vê a frente do Japão, está completamente enganado. Falando de brasileiro, deixe eu ver o que está acontecendo com aquele tonto.

Roncando? Durma com os anjos, meu amor.

Tirar gaijin tooroku / Tirar o modelo 19

Alice é a primeira vez que um cliente meu dorme no telefone. Devo tá com algum problema. Esquece isso. Como estava dizendo, o brasileiro chega no Japão e só

vê a superfície brilhante, a tecnologia de Primeiro Mundo, ruas limpas, pessoas educadas. E tá cheio de gente, logo, ele é como um peixe nadando num cardume de superfícies. Ele perde o senso da realidade, perde seu know-how brasileiro. Ele é um inocente caído em outro planeta. Em São Paulo, ele podia sentir o batedor de carteira do seu lado, ele podia reconhecer o policial disfarçado no outro lado do bar. Aqui em Tokyo, ele é um índio nu. Esse índio acha que se ficar um pouco mais, o que está dentro da superfície ficará aparente no final mas o que acontece é que o que está dentro vai mais pro fundo ainda. O brasileiro fala muito, pensando que se comunica. Para o japonês, não é uma questão de

comunicação, é uma questão de leitura. Ai, o telefone de novo.

Ela foi vista almoçando com bicheiros.

Falar em katakana

Moshi moshi. *Páginas Verde-Amarelas!* Criando linhas de comunicação. Sucesso nas pontas dos seus dedos. Como posso lhe ser útil? Você é tradutor? Você traduz de japonês para português ou português para japonês? 2,000 kanji. Que sofrimento, meu bem. Não leio muito mas me viro em katakana.[2] Katakana é o que interessa para os estrangeiros de qualquer modo. Um momento, por favor. Tem uma chamada na outra linha. Com licença.

Selecionar furyo / Retirar partes defeituosas

Alice, você vê todos esses japoneses lendo. Eles são o povo mais alfabetizado do mundo. Eles estão constantemente lendo tudo, em todo lugar. Você vê eles lendo nos trens, todos lendo em pé, grudados uns nos outros, lendo. Mesmo que não tenham um jornal ou gibi eles são forçados a ler os anúncios em volta. Olha em volta. Me

---

[2] Um sistema de caracteres silábicos destinado principalmente para se escrever palavras estrangeiras e sons e ensinar crianças.

cansa. Eles vivem dentro de um livro. Um livro de piadas! E somos parte dele. Quando eles te olham, eles te lêem. Eles te lêem com os olhos, os narizes, os nervos. Eles te cheiram, te degustam, te desmontam e te reconstróem. E

何時頃お戻りになりますか。

isso pode acontecer numa troca de drinks ou num simples cumprimento. Eles são cheios de informação mas vazios de conversa. Por outro lado, os brasileiros não tem paciência para ler; eles só falam. É por isso que esse negócio por telefone dá dinheiro. Eu devia saber. Ai meu Deus, esqueci do meu cliente . . .

Uma coleção de fotos exclusivas não publicadas anteriormente estão na última edição da Playboy.

Wasuretar / Esquecer

Desculpe mas, tem tanto trabalho aqui hoje! Estou sozinha no escritório. Mas me diga uma coisa, vocês também têm serviços para pagar hoken[3] e shaken?[4] Maravilha. Dá tanto trabalho que é melhor pagar alguém prá fazer isso. Se você quiser colocar um anúncio, põe tudo que quiser nele. Diga que você tem um serviço de consultoria. Você traduz, interpreta, faz hoken e shaken, et cetera, et cetera. Pois é claro que seu negócio vai dar certo. O Japão é o país das oportunidades. Conheço um cara em Nagoya que construiu um império com três restaurantes, um negócio de importação / exportação e um supermercado. Ele fez tudo isso em sete anos, e como ele começou? Com nada mais do que sete marmitas. Isso mesmo. Tope a parada. Posso arranjar isso sem problema. Pode me mandar seu anúncio por fax. De nada. Às ordens.

Levar um hanashi / Levar um papo

Alice, consegui outro anúncio para as Páginas. Você sabe que todos esses jornais fazem dinheiro vendendo anúncios. Pense nisso. Se cada anúncio custa go-ju-man en,[5] acrescente isso. Eu não sou diferente. Você acha que o brasileiro está lendo jornais? Claro que não. No máximo ele lê as manchetes e ponto final. Se a manchete não manchar na página provavelmente ele nem presta atenção. Talvez ele procure por um velho conhecido que desapareceu, anúncios de empreiteira e horóscopo. É um jogo para ver se ele pode ler o futuro. Esse jornais são um grande horóscopo dekassegui. Eles falam quem ele é e quem ele será.. Deixe eu ver se aquele dorminhoco ainda está na outra linha.

---

[3] Seguro   [4] Inspeção de carro   [5] 500.000 ienes

Para uma versão completa de seu vídeo, Numa Cama de Pétalas de Cerejeira, ligue para a Locadora Futurama—(0276)62-1536.

Ainda dormindo? Tá cansado, coitadinho. Ótimo.

Estar tudo daijobu / Estar tudo bem

Alice? Não, ele não está morto. Eu tou escutando ele roncar. Meu Deus! Como eu estava dizendo, os jornais são um enorme horóscopo dekassegui. Um jornal só fala sobre dekasseguis mortos, por suicídio, acidentes de carro e acidentes no trabalho. As páginas sangram com o sangue dos dekassegui. Um outro jornal fala sobre as estórias de sucesso dos dekassegui, dekasseguis que ficaram ricos com seus investimentos, no Brasil. Outro jornal mostra como os dekasseguis podem obter sucesso no Japão abrindo clubes e shopping centers. Outro jornal informa que o Brasil é um desastre econômico, que o crime só piora, o dekassegui que voltou com dinheiro e foi assaltado no mesmo dia. O pobre deka não tem chance. Ele não pode voltar para casa a não ser que seja rico o suficiente para assegurar seus bens. Implica em muita vontade e muita sorte para não dizer um milagre. É mesmo, meu bêbado dorminhoco.

Para a voz dela gravada em êxtase, disque (052) 331-0354.

Fazer zangyo / Fazer hora extra

Alô meu príncipe adormecido. O que foi? Um beijo para acordar? Eu fiquei aqui o tempo todo te esperando. Como poderia te abandonar? Além disso você estava roncando com tanto gosto. Aí eu pensei: ele está cansado, Maria. Deixe ele descansar. Quanto tempo? Talvez uns 10 minutos. 15? Quem sabe? Eu tenho bastante paciência. Seu tempo? Olhe aqui, nunca ninguém dormiu com a Maria Maravilha! Estou é muito ofendida. Você é um cara de pau. Eu te liguei? Além de tudo você estava falando no seu sono. O que você disse? Guarde isso para outra vez. Tchau.

Alice, eu estou te contando isso confidencialmente para deixar com você a verdadeira história da minha vida. Os jornais só fazem fofoca. Tudo vira um escândalo sem nenhuma prova. Eles já estão falando tanta besteira sobre mim; as mentiras não são nem um pingo interessantes. Meu fofoqueiro traduziu para o fofoqueiro deles como se fossem fatos reais. Informação exclusiva. O que vale é a manchete, a entrevista exclusiva. Minha vida parece uma mentira. Quem quer ouvir a verdade? Ai, o telefone de novo.

Para a imagem holográfica dela num chaveiro, disque (075) 255-5520.

Ue, sugoi ne? / Uau, é surpreendente, não é?

*Belo adormecido, voltou? Eu ia dizer, há homens que ficam de
pau duro quando dormem. É verdade? Eu? Meus peitinhos
estão durinhos. Minha bucetinha—molhadinha. Entre você e
eu, a gente podia transar durante nosso sono. Em nossos sonhos. Sua memória me enche, incha no meio das minhas per-*

*nas, expulsa uma ou outra
memória, violenta e suave. Qual é o
problema? Querido, é só poesia.
Bem, se a Cida pode te dar mais
prazer, então ligue prá ela.Tô pouco
me lixando.*

Alice, eu não sei o que está acontecendo hoje.Tô perdendo o meu
jeito. De qualquer maneira os
meus dias estão contados nesse
telefone. O futuro é na sua Cafénette. Esses homens todos
vão me abandonar por uma mulher virtual. Até lá, o deka
vê minha foto na primeira página do International Press.
É claro que eles arrancam a página que tem meu corpo
sensual mas isso não interessa. Meu rosto diz tudo. Meu
desejo vai prá dentro da calça dele e ele só pensa em sexo
e dinheiro. Se ele pudesse me ter, é verdade, ele poderia ter
o mundo. Mas não se esqueça do segredo deste mundo:
honne / tatemae.Agora você me vê. Agora você não me vê.

Zero Zero One-derful

業

Maria Madalena Oliveira Shinbashi, artistic dancer, age 28, native of São Paulo, was last seen in Roppongi at the Saci Pereré in Shinjuku. A warrant for her arrest is outstanding. Any information about her whereabouts should be directed to the police department of Tokyo City.

dar um sampo / to take a walk

Listen girl, it's truer than the truth even if no one will ever believe me. It was a lovely night in May. I can see it now, like yesterday: one gorgeous full moon dancing in the ocean, jumping the waves like a white rabbit. And me, like a fool, running after it. No, no, Alice, in those days I was a total virgin. Okay, maybe I got a whiff of marijuana. This was innocent revelry. Hold on. Someone's on the other line. Let me settle this account, and I'll be back in a minute.

Hello, Maria Maravilha at your service. Who? Oh yes, I recognize your voice. Of course. I always remember the voice of a handsome man. Oh well, what does it matter if you've never called me before. There's always a first time, no? After all, it's all about pretending. It won't do you any good if you don't have a good imagination. Wait just one moment. I'm going to pick this line up in my bedroom. Okay?

estar hantai /
to be upside down

Alice, there's a guy on the other line, but he can wait. As I was saying, I was jumping around in the ocean like a kid free of any cares when suddenly I fell into a hole, a vortex, going down like a piece of shit. There wasn't time to be surprised. I thought it was the end. You're laughing? This is God's honest truth. Wait a minute.

Maria Madalena Yoshiwara Shinbashi, sex worker, age 32, native of Curitiba, was last seen on May 5 at the Paraiso Latino in Kawasaki City with drummer Alexandre Ozaki. Ozaki, questioned by investigators, stated that Shinbashi did not seem to have any immediate plans. Her disappearance was not expected. Shinbashi is thought to be associated with the disappearance of funds to be disbursed to employees under contract through her Tudo Daijobu human resources business in the amount of 5.5 million yen.

ser mattaku japonês / gaijin / to be a bona fide Japanese / foreigner

Hello. That's better. I'm in my bedroom now. We can speak freely here. Let's see. We were talking about your imagination. Well now, you can imagine whatever you please. My hair for example. What color do you like? You guessed it. I'm blonde all the way. You don't believe me? The photo in the newspaper?

Maybe that's not my photo. They can print any photo they want. Well, they should use a photo of a blonde. The Japanese love blondes. You're not Japanese? Of course not. You're Brazilian. Where are you from? Mato Grosso do Sul? So far away. I don't know that part of the country, but they say it's beautiful. I want to hear all about it, but I'm dying for a cold beer. How about you? Good. I'll be right back.

Madalena Shinbashi of Rio de Janeiro and Tokyo was known to be a former performer and hostess in Shinjuku. She subsequently started a contractual employment business and was famous for being the first and so far only contractor imprisoned for her activities.

Cair do tatami / to fall out of bed

Alice, he's just a boy on the other line. I feel so sorry for him. Far away from his mom. I'm going to have to give him a big treat. That's the way I am. I fall in love with all my clients. But returning to our conversation, I fell into the

curl of a wave that slipped down, down, right to the center of the earth, but I must have gone into shock. Maybe I fell asleep. I completely lost all sense of time. How could

お言づけお願い出来ますか。

I lie about a thing like this? One day I was home; the next, I woke up here. Wouldn't you know it. The third line is ringing. Hold on a minute.

Moshi moshi. *Páginas Verde-Amarelas!* The only telephone book in Japan published for Brazilians! How may I direct your call? Ah Carlinhos, you're just the person I needed to hear from. Well, as you know, this year we are enlarging the *Páginas*. Not only will we have all the new businesses opening in Japan, but we are interested in offering the best service possible, understand? For example, you'll be able to use our coupons to get discounts. I think this would be a good idea for you, to give discounts to customers who subscribe to your telephone service. You've already got a quarter-page announcement, but how about investing a little more in a postcard insert? I can fax you an example. Carlinhos, you'll have to excuse me. There's a customer on another line. To tell you the truth, it's your competition, IDC, International Digital Communications. But don't worry. I'll be back in a moment, but I'm pretty sure he wants a full-page announcement. I could be wrong.

Maria Maravilha Shinbashi, resident of Roppongi, has disappeared and is accused of absconding with funds earmarked for payment to employees. Her business partner, Zé Maria Fukuyama, denies being an accomplice in the theft of the missing funds, said to be approximately 55 million yen. He expressed surprise that his partner Shinbashi had suddenly disappeared.

fazer kampai / to make a toast

Oh honey, have you got your cold beer? Are you comfortable? So where were we? Mato Grosso do Sul. You know

that I'm from Rio? It's been so long since I've been home. How long have you been here? Only two years? Wait till you've been here seven like me. Oh, you never get used to it. You came alone? What about that girlfriend you left behind? Oh no, tell me about it. How sad. Of course she still loves you. Forever is forever. And your mother? Of course you can't tell her how bad it is for you here, but then she's your mother. You'll get back home again. It's just a matter of time. Of course you'll see her alive again. It's really all right to cry. Go ahead. Let it all out. You're making me cry too. Let me get a tissue.

Maria Madalena Shinbashi is presumed to be in the Bahamas.

ser mulher do obento / to be a lunchbox lady

Alice, are you still there? My client's crying his eyes out. I'll explain later, but, at this rate, I'll never be able to tell you anything. What are you doing? Frying? Bife à milanesa? How many? One hundred? Who'd have predicted that you'd become an obento lady? Don't forget that I got you your first job. Well, go on with your cooking. I'll be back.

Carlos, gomen, ne. The competition is tough, huh? As I was saying, a half-page for IDC. Come on. Why don't you buy an entire page or even two. I've heard that Brazilians spend 4 billion yen per year in international telephone calls. And KDD is the largest telephone company in Japan.

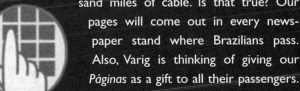

They say that you have two hundred thousand miles of cable. Is that true? Our pages will come out in every newspaper stand where Brazilians pass. Also, Varig is thinking of giving our Páginas as a gift to all their passengers. Dekasegis will disembark with it. You're a telephone business, and we're the telephone book. We help you expand your business. What more do you want? But one moment please. I have another call. You see? They are all clamoring to announce with us.

KAREN TEI YAMASHITA

Baby, baby. Are you all right? Don't be embarrassed. That's why I'm here for you. Can you feel my voice with you? Does it help? My lips are so close to your ear. If I stick my tongue out, I can taste the salt on the very tip. There. I can feel you through the phone. Tell me what you feel. Oh really? Well then, I'll have to change. You know that I've just come home. I'm in these really tight jeans. Let me slip out of them. You'll hold for me won't you? Hold for me, baby.

ser deka / to be a dekasegi

Carlinhos, have you decided? While you've been deciding, I've sold two more ads. Let me tell you something. What you pay me only covers the cost. This is a work of love. I don't earn a cent. Think about it. What the dekasegi lacks is information. He's an animal completely without knowledge about Japan, of the language, the customs, connections. Poor guy. You think the consulate is there to help? Not much. We have to alleviate this situation. How many Brazilians have told me personally that the *Páginas Verde-Amarelas!* have been the most useful publication that they've encountered. And that's not just one or two but dozens. They are all awaiting the new edition. This time we have a provision of fifty thousand copies. The last time, we did twenty-five thousand, and in one week we sold everything. We had to print another ten thousand, and it still wasn't enough. If you invest a little more, maybe we can do a little more. But hold the line again.

Alice, how goes the cooking? And rice? Is it ready? I'm so hungry! What about your plans to start an internet cafe? What did you want to call it? Cafénette? Guys come to eat, drink, and spend a little time on the internet. Well, you already have the kitchen. All you need is to add tables. Your biggest investment is going to be computers, but I know you have the money. Hold on again.

I'm back, sweetheart. I'm sorry to keep you waiting. I put on something pink and very transparent. Use your imagination. And a special perfume, an aphrodisiac wouldn't you know? It drives me crazy with desire. I put on some red red lipstick as well. My lips are on fire. You don't sound very enthusiastic. Still sad, thinking about mother? Don't get mad, dear. I know you pay by the minute, but it isn't necessary to be gross about it. A woman has her preparations, don't you know? With me, you can't just pull it out, get it in, come, and get on with business. There's a ritual to this. You need to learn your manners, dear. Well, when you're ready, give me a call. I'll be here. Tchau.

好評発売中

Maria Madalena Shinbashi is said to be in Bali.

wakatar / to understand

Okay, Carlinhos, I'm going to accept your request. The deal is closed. You get several pages with postcard inserts for KDD. You are going to see how many new subscriptions you get through our pages. No, no. No more discussions about this. You've convinced me entirely. I know how difficult things have become with the business of callback. We've already got ten ads for callback[1] companies. Think of it! Callback is half the price of KDD! The poor Brazilian spends all his salary on the telephone, but that's another conversation. I'm helping you out, of course. I'll send you a contract tomorrow. Leave it to me. You are doing this for business but also to serve the community. If we don't do this, who will? I'm tired of treating Brazilians in Japan like they're helpless. Their biggest problem is the language, and these pages translate into basic survival tools. Tchau, Carlinhos. Look for my fax.

She has stashed the money in a bank account in Singapore.

Sair do teiji / to leave the routine

Alice, now then, for just a moment I'm free from busi-

ness. Where was I? Falling into that hole and then fainting, right? So, when I finally opened my eyes, there I was in a bed of cherry blossoms, surrounded by a sweet perfume, in an oh-so-soft bed, blossoms falling all around. I thought I had died, but when I really looked, I was actually under a bunch of lights and cameras. There was an

じゃ、また電話します。

electric fan blowing the petals all over and an old director with a baseball cap yelling directions. And, as if that wasn't enough, I was stark naked. I must have lost my bikini in the fall. It was horrible. My hair felt glued together like seaweed, my breasts and butt peppered with sand and pieces of seashells. It wasn't a dream. No way. I was as awake as I am this very moment. I swear. Do you think I'm a schizophrenic or what do they call it? Oh, here we go again. Another call.

ser karaoquiero / to be a karaoke singer

Moshi moshi. *Páginas Verde-Amarelas!* Here to help Brazilians in the best way possible. How may I direct your call? We consider the *Páginas* a service to the community. We are going to publish all the numbers of Brazilian businesses without question. Beauty salons, schools, bars, export / import, contractors, tourist agencies,

---

[1] International long-distance telephone operation: caller dials a station in U.S. that "calls back" making connection to Brazil but charging only the distance / rate between U.S. and Brazil.

73

meat-by-mail, hostess services. We publish it all. What sort of business do you do? Karaoqueiro? Of course we want to include performers like you. Why not? Musicians, capoeira players, drummers, singers. Now if you're interested in an ad other than just your telephone  number, there will be a small charge. But if you can invest a little more, it would be to your advantage I'm sure, and you'd help us meet our publishing costs. We Brazilians need a communications network. Once you are part of this network, you will find greater possibilities for life here. A person like you with special talent deserves a better chance. How about an eighth-page ad with your photograph? Wonderful. You'll see. Nothing to be gained without a little investment. I'll be sending you a contract in the mail, okay?

Sources say she has stashed the money in a bank account in Bangkok.

estar tudo barabara / to be all jumbled up

Alice, I've already sold several pages of ads today. But, back to my story. Me naked running around crazy. No escape. The camera chasing after me. The film won awards at Cannes. I was completely convincing of course. That's how I arrived in Japan—it was a complete accident—without documents, not even a hanky to cover me. Shameful! Makes me cry just to remember. Maybe

there are others who've arrived like me, but we've never met. You and the others arrived normally by Varig, Vasp, KAL, and JAL. Even so, you all arrived naked too. Naked metaphorically of course. In my case, it's all recorded on film. Here comes another client.

Investigators are looking into reports that she deposited funds in a bank account in Vancouver.

gambatear / to persevere

Hello? Who is it? Sérgio? It's hard to hear you darling. Where are you? A train station? At a pay phone? Yes, this is Maria Maravilha. Of course that's my real name. No I can't meet you. You've got a hard-on have you? How hard? Oh really? Oh, tell me more. Where did you say you are? Impossible. I'm in Tokyo. Why don't you call me back from someplace where, you know, I can alleviate your tension? You live with six other guys? Oh yeah, that's such a drag. If you came to Tokyo? Oh no, you'd never find me. Don't even bother, love. Oh-oh, your phone card's running out . . .

Alice, are the beans ready? I'm dying for beans. Who'd have thought you'd get domesticated like this? Of course you were a mother with kids, but I bet you never cooked in those days; it was either your mother or the maid. You always talk about your arrival here as the beginning of a new life. Liberating is the word you use. Ha! Okay, it's true that your ex-husband in Brazil was a hopeless drunk,

It's my pink phone again. It's usually only busy on the weekends. I shouldn't complain; it pays the bills.

Reports state that she has a bank account in Port-au-Prince.

estar genqui / to be well

Hello? Oh, so you decided to call me back? Me mad? Well, a little. Do you get in fights with your girlfriend? Do you start the

じゃ、また電話します。

fights or does she? Who's the jealous one? She is? Well maybe she should be jealous. Do you call her often? Every week? Haven't you been calling me every week? That's not you? I could have sworn. Do you and your girlfriend get it on on the phone? Well, you should. Oh I see. Well, you have something to look forward to, ne? I agree one hundred percent. Talking on the phone is entirely harmless. Safe sex. I wouldn't have it any other way. The rich and famous do it all the time. President Clinton, Diana … Of course, call me anytime. Maria Maravilha will always be at your disposal.

Alice, why don't you put an ad in the *Páginas*? I'll give you a discount. Call your business Alice's Cafénette. Enjoy a beer with pastel while you surf the net. Maybe we could put the *Páginas* online with a website. I hear you can make a mint off the advertising. Another call. Well, I shouldn't complain. Still, the money could be better.

Moshi moshi. *Páginas Verde-Amarelas!* Introducing Brazilians to the Japanese communications network. How may I direct your call? Ana? You aren't working for the *Jornal Tudo Bem* anymore? I bet you've moved to *International Press* then. No? To *Folha Mundial*? When? Well, I have a proposal. You buy an ad for your paper in the *Páginas* and I'll buy an ad in your paper. A trade. This way we help the *Folha*, and you help the *Páginas*. Ads for ads. Done deal. Ana, you must know about these new magazines like *Made in Japan* and *Aqui Japão*. How about cable TV? I'm trying to convince them to put in ads with us. Could you share your contacts? Great. I owe you one. Tchau.

She has been seen with unsavory characters.

falar de keitai / to talk by cellphone

Who's speaking? Marcelo? Oh you're a very nasty man. Where are you? I can hear machinery. It's a factory isn't it? You're on break? You can't blame me for your being distracted. Who pasted my photo to that gearshaft? You could

lose a finger? My fault? But you haven't lost any fingers or your dick for that matter! Oh honey, heavy machinery turns me on too. Let's get this over with. Are you on your cellphone? Well, find a place and call me back.

Alice, I know you don't believe in my story, but there's no explanation. I didn't lose my memory. I arrived without a visa or a passport, without any kind of information. New life, honey! I started from zero. I had to do it all alone.

Learned the language by myself. There are Brazilians here some seven years who still don't know more than to ask for the toilet. They arrive here thinking that life owes them something. Oh, here's another one—

Marcelo? Where are you? In a toilet stall? It's totally crude, but for you, I'm in there too. I'm going to suck you dry, so you can't blame me for anything ever. Promise? No, you've got to promise. Okay, are you listening? Are you unzipped? Hello? Hello?

Alice, I got cut off. I think my client dropped his cell-phone in the toilet. I've got another call for the *Páginas*. Stop laughing.

She was seen with members of a Colombian drug cartel.

shigotar / to work

Moshi, moshi. *Páginas Verde-Amarelas!* Working to help Brazilians realize their dreams. How may I direct your call? Our scheduled publication date is August. Of course we'd like to align the publication date with the August festivals in order to attract attention in the community. For example, we'll be at the Samba Matsuri in Oizumi. An excellent opportunity to promote the *Páginas*. There are over three hundred Brazilian businesses active today in Japan. And the number increases every day. The new *Páginas* will triple in size. If we leave only a hundred copies of the *Páginas* in every store, that's thirty thousand *Páginas* to furnish. Think of it! The *Páginas* represent the surface of an extensive Brazilian business network in Japan. Now, without a doubt, you, as an empreiteira, will want to be tied to this enormous resource. The first thing on any dekasegi's mind is always to find work. A half-page? Wonderful. I'll fax you our contract. Very simple, without complications. Thank you for your business.

estar de yaquin / to be on night duty

Alice, since I arrived here, I've had a special education. My first job was as a hostess in a high-class karaoke bar in Roppongi. They offered sake with small tissues of gold floating on top. Besides gold, who knows what other substances they played with? I tried to keep my nose clean. I had to be smarter than they thought I was, had to learn how to keep awake. I wasn't going to fall into another hole. Who knows where I'd end up? You think you can be awake for only a certain amount of time, but Tokyo keeps you up longer: you can be awake forever in an endless dream. Hold on.

Hello? Is that so? You sound like you've been tipping the bottle. Of course not. I'm having a beer right now myself. Relax, I say. Japan is too uptight. I know what you mean. Don't you miss just hanging out at the corner bar, snacking on fries and olives, soaking in the afternoon sun, shooting the breeze? I know what you mean. I could always find my daddy at the corner bar in the afternoons, playing cards, throwing dice. Tell me about your favorite hangout. Tell me. Hello? Oh . . .

She was reported seen with Bolivian drug dealers.

tsukaretar / to get tired

Alice, my client fell asleep. He pays me by the minute, but he's sleeping like a fool. He works overtime just to phone me in his free time. He could pachinkar,[2] but he'd rather call me. The rest of his money he sends to his mother in Goiânia. Yell for him to wake up? Not me. Leave him in peace.

But as I was saying, the world beneath the streets of Tokyo is perpetually turned on, oxygen pumped in, carbon monoxide pumped out. Its guts are a twisting Godzilla breathing for you. In this underworld inside Japan, I learned to live Japanese. Anyone ever told you about honne / tatemae? It's what's inside and what's outside. It's what you don't see and what you see. The Brazilian never learns this, but it's essential to know for life here. He thinks that what he sees is the thing itself, but the Japanese never see anything that way. For the Japanese, everything can be something else. Everything can change. Everything has a true inside and a front that covers it. Even the face of something can be in question. I've got myself a blue telephone, see, but this will never be clear to the Japanese. He'll say: maybe it's blue. Could it be blue? Possibly it's blue. Is it really blue? What is blue? Shall we agree that it is blue? The Brazilian who sees only the face of Japan is completely fooled. Speaking of the Brazilian, let me check up on the fool.

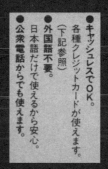

Snoring? Sleep with angels, my love.

tirar gaijin tooroku / to get an alien registration card

Alice, a client has never gone to sleep on me. I must be losing it. Oh forget it. As I was saying, the Brazilian arrives in Japan and only sees the brilliant surface, the technology of the first world, clean streets, educated people. And it's crowded, so he's like a fish swimming in a school of surfaces. He loses his sense of reality, loses his Brazilian know-how. He's an innocent

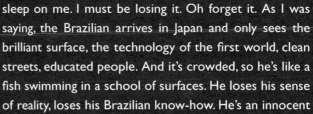

---

[2] to play pachinko, a gambling pinball game

fallen to another planet. In São Paulo, he could feel the pickpocket at his side; he could recognize the undercover man on the other side of the bar. Here in Tokyo, he's one naked Indian. This Indian thinks if he stays a little longer, what's inside the surface will finally become apparent, but that inside only goes down deeper. The Brazilian is full of talk. He reveals his inside with his constant talk, thinking that he is communicating. For the Japanese, it's not a question of communication, it's a question of reading. Oh, there goes the phone again.

She was seen having lunch with lottery kingpins.

falar em katakana /
to speak in katakana
Moshi moshi. *Páginas Verde-Amarelas!* Creating lines of communication. Success is at the tip of your fingers. How may I direct your call? You're a translator? Do you translate Japanese to Portuguese or Portuguese to Japanese? Two thousand kanji. What a pain, honey. I don't read much, but I can manage the katakana. Katakana is what matters to foreigners anyway. One moment please. I have a call on another line. Excuse me.

selecionar furyo / to remove faulty parts
Alice, you see all these Japanese reading. They're the most literate people in the world. They are constantly reading, everything everywhere. You see them in trains, all reading standing up, crushed together reading. Even if

they haven't got a paper or a comic book, they read the advertisements that surround them. Look around. It tires me out. They live inside a book. A comic book! And you are part of it. When they look at you, they read you. They read you with their eyes, noses, nerves. They smell you, taste you, take you apart and reconstruct you. And all this can happen in the exchange of a drink, in a simple bow. They are full of information but empty of talk. On the other hand, Brazilians have no patience for reading; they only want to talk. That's why this telephone business makes money. I should know. Oh my god, I forgot about my client—

A collection of her exclusive previously unpublished photos are in the latest issue of Playboy.

---

wasuretar / to forget
I'm so sorry, but it's so busy here today. I'm here all alone in the office. But tell me, do you also provide services to pay hoken[3] and shaken?[4] Wonderful. It's so much trouble that you ought to be able to pay someone to do it. If you want to put in an ad, describe everything you do. Say that

---

[3] insurance   [4] car inspection

78

you have a consulting business. You translate, interpret, consult, do hoken and shaken, et cetera, et cetera. Of course your business is going to take off. Japan is a land of opportunities. I know a guy in Nagoya who's built an empire with three restaurants, an import / export business, and a supermarket. He did this all in seven years, and how did he start out? With nothing but seven box lunches! That's right. Take the plunge. Very good. I can set that up for you easily. You can fax me your notice. Not at all. At your service.

levar um hanashi / to have a conversation

Alice, I got another ad for the *Páginas*. You know that all these newspapers make their money by selling ads. Think of it. If each ad costs about go-ju-man[5] en, add it up. I'm no different. You think the Brazilian is reading the papers? Of course not. He's looking at the headlines, and that's about it. If the headline doesn't bleed on the page, he probably doesn't pay much attention. Maybe he looks for an old acquaintance now disappeared, the empreiteira ads, and his horoscope. It's a game to see if he can read the future. These newspapers are a big dekasegi horoscope. They tell him who he is and who he will be.

KAREN TEI YAMASHITA

Let me check in on that sleeper on the other line.

For the unedited version of her video, Numa Cama de Pétalas de Cerejeira, *call Locadora Futurama at (0276) 62-1536.*

Still sleeping? So tired, poor thing. Beautiful.

estar tudo daijobu / to be okay

Alice? No, he isn't dead. I can hear him snoring. My god! But like I was saying, the newspapers are a big dekasegi horoscope. One paper only talks about dead dekasegi: by suicide, car fatalities, work accidents. The pages bleed

何時頃お戻りになりますか。

with the blood of dekasegi. Another paper talks about dekasegi success stories, dekasegi who've become rich with their investments in Brazil. Another paper shows how dekasegi can obtain success in Japan by opening clubs and shopping malls. Another paper tells you that Brazil is an economic disaster, that the crime only gets worse, and about the dekasegi who returned with money and was robbed in the same day. The poor deka doesn't have a chance. He can't return home unless he's rich enough to secure his goods. It takes a great will and a lot of luck, if not a miracle. Oh right, my sleeping drunkard.

---

[5] 500.000 yen

fazer zangyo / to do overtime

Hello my sleeping prince. How about it? A kiss to wake? I've been here all the time waiting for you. How could I abandon you? Besides which you were snoring with such gusto. I thought: he's tired, Maria, let him rest. How long? Maybe ten minutes? Fifteen? Who knows. I've plenty of patience. Your time? Look here, no one has ever gone to sleep on Maria Maravilha! I'm very offended. You have some nerve. Did I call you? Besides, you were talking in your sleep. What did you say? Save that for another time, darling. Tchau.

Alice, I'm telling you this in confidence, to leave my true history in your keeping. The newspapers are only gossip. Everything turns into a scandal without any proof. They're already saying so much nonsense about me; the lies aren't even interesting. My hearsay translated into their hearsay into facts on the page. Exclusive information. What matters is the headline, the exclusive interview. My life reads like a big lie. Who wants to hear the truth? Oh, the persistence of this phone!

Ue, sugoi ne? / wow, amazing isn't it?

Sleeping beauty, back again? I was going to say, there are men who get hard when they sleep. Is that so? Me? My nipples get hard. My crotch gets wet. Between you and me, we could do it in our sleep. In our dreams. Your memory fills me, swells between my thighs, chokes away every other memory, violent and tender. What's the matter? Darling, it's just poetry. Well, if Cida can get you off better, then call Cida. I really don't care.

Alice, I don't know what it is today. I'm losing my touch. In any case, my days on this phone are numbered. The future is in your Cafénette. These men will all be abandoning me for a woman in cyber. Until then, the deka sees my photo on the first page of the *International Press*. Of course they crop out my naked sensuous body, but no matter. My face says everything. My desire reaches into his pants, and he thinks about nothing but sex and money. If he could have me, it's true, he could have the world. But don't forget the secret of this world: honne / tatemae: Now you see me, now you don't.

June: Circle K Recipes

米

Gohan

Wash rice until the water runs clear. For each cup of rice, add a cup of water. Place in rice cooker, and push the button.

Arroz

Rinse rice and drain. Sauté chopped garlic, onion, and salt in oil. Add rice and sauté. Add water. For each cup of rice, add about 2 cups of water. Bring to a boil. Lower heat and cover until tender. (If you live in Japan, dump the sautéed rice into the rice cooker, add water, and push the button.)

ONE DAY, AT A RESTAURANT THAT SPECIALIZES IN tofu, I heard the people at the next table ordering "raisu." "Raisu, hitotsu."[1] I thought I had misunderstood, but after I could read the katakana on menus, I got it. That you can order rice at a Japanese restaurant seems obvious, but that it's called "rice" is one of those things in Japan that has a reason you can only guess. My guess is that the word *kome* means rice, the grain; and the word *gohan* also means rice, but refers to food generally as well. There's no word for just an extra bowl of rice. So, *raisu*. But, in the old days, if you were eating food (gohan), you were eating rice (gohan).

My grandfather came from the small village of Naegi, which has been incorporated into the larger city of Nakatsugawa, in Gifu Prefecture. His family apparently owned enough land to parcel a portion out to tenants who paid in rice. In those days, rice was legal tender. A large storehouse used to stand where the family turned that rice into sake. My father once speculated that the fall of his family may have come about from *drinking* that legal tender. Recently, the family who now owns and farms the land in Naegi sent us a large sack of rice produced on that very land. *Naegi no okome.* I washed and cooked several cups of it very carefully, and we all ate it, trying to taste each grain. It was an odd little ritual, like eating your ancestors. Or eating legal tender.

---

[1] one bowl of rice

I was born in the year of the rabbit. On evenings with a full moon, I look up to find the outline of a rabbit pounding rice into the giant omochi that is, they say, the moon. When I was a child, my grandmother stuck a few grains of rice to the lobes of my ears. I always thought my ears were too big, but she said they were good luck; if you can stick rice to your lobes, you'll be rich. Kanemochi.[2] The sticky rice knows. Legal tender here.

In Japan, rice must be sticky and polished white. One eats the purity of it. It doesn't matter if its nutrition is negligible. You can rarely find any other sort of rice, or grain for that matter. No brown rice. No barley. No cracked wheat. No cornmeal. No long grain. A Brazilian woman explained the difference between the short and long grains: "Japanese rice: Juntos venceremos! / Together we will succeed! Brazilian rice: Sozinho, consigo! / I can do it myself!"

And heaven forbid that the Japanese should eat the long-grain rice of Thailand.

Everyone can tell you how Thai rice was introduced into the Japanese market only to be given a bad rep and thrown away by the tons. They complained: It had a funny smell. Someone found a piece of insect in it. It wasn't sticky. It was cheap. It was just a food staple from a poor country. In that sense, it wasn't rice. It wasn't legal tender. Who's eating it now? Probably the Brazilians.

☺

It's the rainy season in Japan. Water fills the rice paddies across the countryside. Houses, mini-marts, and factories encroach upon the planted land, replacing the fields gradually, but nothing yet replaces the reign of rice. It's rare in some parts of the country to see gardens of vegetables or fruits. And rarer still are corn, beans, cover crops, or other grains. From the looks of the supermarket offerings, variety and quantity are sacrificed for an almost cloned perfection in the produce. For example, every eggplant looks like every other eggplant. The same goes for cucumbers, tomatoes, onions, potatoes, apples, oranges, melons, etc. Someone produced the incredible statistic that Japan throws away imperfect vegetables and fruits in quantities that equal the weight of the total production of rice each year. You pay for this statistic:

1 tomato = $1.00
1 apple = $1.00
1 head of lettuce = $2.00
1/4 head of nappa cabbage = $1.50
20 lbs rice = $40.00

Although food (gohan) is rice (gohan), obviously rice is not really food. Certainly it is also sake, nuka, roof thatching, paper, glue, starch, matting, and, in the past, foot gear and raincoats. But beyond these by-products, its production, its purity, its mythic qualities, its value, define every

[2] to have money

other thing called food. Everything is measured against it. Legal tender. The stubbornness of rice. The persistence of rice. The gold standard was abolished years ago, but not the rice standard.

Miso-shiru

Bring a pot of water with dashi to boil. Add a scoop of miso paste, and chopped vegetables, seaweed, mushrooms, or tofu.

Feijão

Separate the beans from any pebbles or insects. Wash and soak. Cook in pressure cooker until tender. In a separate pan, sauté onions, garlic, and salt in oil or fat. Smash a cup of the cooked beans into this mixture to make a thickening paste; then stir everything back into the cooked beans. Salt and pepper to taste.

Rice and beans. Arroz e feijão. Inseparable. For Brazilians, the only food that sustains. When the early Japanese immigrants to Brazil arrived on coffee plantations in the twenties, they received a ration of rice, beans, salt, coffee, and sugar. Sugar has always been plentiful in Brazil, and in those days the Japanese knew only to add it to the beans. After several weeks of the sweet stuff, the salty fare must have been a pleasant surprise. In any case, rice and beans became an accepted staple, the food that defines the

people, the daily blessing, a comida sagrada. If gohan (and probably miso soup) is food to Japanese, arroz e feijão is gohan to Brazilians.

Thanks to this cultivation of the Brazilian palate, the first commercial ventures among Brazilians in Japan have been related to the making and sale of Brazilian food. What is it that the food of your homeland, of your mother's kitchen, will provide you? Why do we crave it so badly? Why do our tongues pull us home? Was mom's cooking really that good? When Japanese immigrants got to Brazil, they spent much of their years laboring to make vegetables, tofu, miso, and shoyu. Now, the dekasegi in Japan finance a lucrative network of imports from Brazil, New Zealand, Australia, and the Philippines to eat the stuff that pleases the literal mother tongue: mandioca, Sonho de Valsa, Guaraná, pão de queijo, linguiça, goiabada, fubá, suco de maracujá.

In the center of every enclave of Brazilian life in Japan, you find food. Sometimes it is a restaurant; sometimes a cantina and grocery store, or a karaoke bar. Sometimes it is a truck stocked with Brazilian goods making designated stops at the lodgings of factory workers in remote towns. Often it is the obento / marmita lady, the woman who delivers box lunches and dinners to factory workers.

The obento lady brings a box lunch with the always dependable arroz e feijão, a piece of meat, and a side of vegetables. The young Brazilian men say that the

Japanese lunches don't "sustain." Rice and pickles don't cut it. They need food that sticks to their ribs. Some don't care for fish. In the first months of their arrival, they all lose weight quickly. The obento lady also brings news, gossip, and motherly advice. Often she's a walking social service; she'll give you information about health insurance, your visa, your driver's license. She's been here a while, started her own business, knows the ropes. Her cellphone rings constantly as she delivers her food. "Carlos, listen, you perforated your lungs once already. Forget the overtime for a while. Give it a rest. Do you hear me?" "Luís? I heard you moved to Toyota. Of course there's a friend of mine over there who makes obento. Do you want her telephone number?"

Arroz e feijão, the daily blessing, the tie that binds. Not just food—a social construct.

Yaki-Niku

Arrange thin slices of filet mignon on a plate with a variety of cut vegetables, tofu, and mushroom. Cook at the table on a hot plate with a little oil. Serve with rice, beer, and sake.

Bife à Milanesa

Pound slices of beef flat. Dip them in egg and bread crumbs and fry. Serve with rice and beans.

About seven years ago, a small butcher shop in the town of Yoro in Gifu put out a flyer offering imported meat from Australia at extraordinarily cheap prices. The flyer attracted several Brazilians who came to buy the meat and who also returned on the following Sunday, despite the fact that the offer was for one week only. The Brazilians peered past the counter and asked about some pieces of meat on the block. This was meat cut away from the fine rib eye or perhaps from the filet that Japanese customers expected to buy, but the Brazilians offered to take this unwanted meat. Every weekend, the Brazilians returned for more meat, for the side cuts and the tougher meats. Finally, the owner found herself too busy to handle these Brazilians and invited them into the shop to cut away the pieces they wanted: picanha, coxão duro, coxão mole, ponta de agulha.

In time, Brazilians came by the busloads, set up barbecue pits in the empty lot on the side of the shop, roasted meat, played music, sang, and danced. The owners covered the empty lot when it became cold and rainy, and the churrasco and the music continued. They gave up trying to sell fancy cuts of fine Hida and Kobe beef at 200 yen / $2.00 per 100 grams, and transformed the business to provide imported Australian meat cheaply for a more voracious clientele, for Brazilians whose families can be counted on to each buy as much as 10 kilos of meat—beef, chicken, pork, bacon, ham, and sausages—per week. Brazilian grocery items were added to the shop. The empty lot turned into a churrascaria restaurant complete with live music and karaoke. Finally it sponsored a soccer team and turned completely Brazilian. Now there are four other such shops in four other cities in Japan, and they also do a mail-order business, shipping meat directly to the homes of individuals in places as far away as Okinawa and Hokkaido. To fill all these orders, 100 tons of meat are shipped from Australia every month.

As for the owners, the husband is Japanese; the wife is Korean. It's one of those Creole situations: Korean Japanese buying Australian meat and selling it in Japan to Brazilians.

Gyoza

Fill gyoza wrappers with a mixture of ground pork and chopped vegetables. Arrange them on a pan, frying them all on one side in a small amount of oil. When browned, spill about a $\frac{1}{4}$ cup of water into the pan, lower heat, cover, and cook until tender.

Pastel

Fill pastel wrappers with cheese, hearts of palm, tomatoes, or ground beef. Fry until crisp and golden.

I learned from my grandmother that after rice, everything else is okazu. At her house, lunch was always a bowl of rice and every jar of tsukemono (pickled vegetables), fermented beans, pickled fish, and salted squid she could bring out of the refrigerator. I imagine okazu is an old term, not used much in Japan today. The Hawaiians still use it; in Hilo, I tried a sushi they call okazu-maki. The Brazilians have a similar term: mistura. Everything after rice and beans is mistura. Gyoza is okazu. Pastel is mistura.

I don't know if anyone has ever done a study of the origins of the pastel in Brazil. I assume the Chinese brought fried wonton to Brazil and adapted it to Brazilian tastes. But it was the Japanese immigrants who became attached to its production, frying it behind stands at the feiras, or open marketplaces. In Brazil, fried wonton became much larger in size. Instead of a pork filling, there is cheese, hearts of palm, tomatoes, or ground beef. The dough is thicker; the secret in the recipe they say is pinga, that most potent of cane brandies. Now pastel is back in Asia, but it is back as *pastel*. It is not Chinese or Korean or even Japanese; it is Brazilian.

☺

We recently visited the very traditional village of Shirakawa, where all the houses are 200 years old and have thatch roofs. Also special to this area is the mountain cooking, which includes fern sprouts, bamboo shoots, and mushrooms gathered from the mountainside. Curious, we visited a factory that packages these mountain veggies because we had heard that a Brazilian family worked there. As it turns out, all the materials for this local specialty are imported from China and Russia, and have been for the last twelve years. To use the local produce would be far too expensive. So there you have it: unknown to thousands of tourists who pass this way, the packages of mountain vegetables bought as omiyage[3] come from China and Russia and are made and packaged by Brazilians.

An Okinawan nutritionist in Yokohama opened a Brazilian restaurant because she noticed that the young Brazilians coming to work in Japan were all losing weight, all seemed to have difficulty eating Japanese food. She wondered about this and went to Brazil to learn to cook Brazilian dishes. Also, a Brazilian cook came to Japan to study Japanese cuisine, and now she is the chef at a Brazilian restaurant in Nagoya whose fine food attracts a clientele both Japanese and Brazilian. A Nikkei whose family traveled from Okinawa to Bolivia to Brazil to Yokohama recently opened her kitchen in Kawasaki, offering both Okinawan and Brazilian dishes. Everybody is making okazu. Everybody is making mistura.

Chawanmushi

Beat eggs and a clear dashi soup together. Place pieces of chicken, gingko nuts, bamboo shoots, mushroom, and fish cake in ceramic cups. Pour egg-soup mixture on top. Steam over boiling water until set. Serve hot in cups.

Pudim

Beat eggs, sweetened condensed milk, and cream in blender. Pour into a pan lined with sugar caramelized with cinnmon and cloves. Steam over boiling water until set. When cool, turn the pudim over onto a plate to serve.

Lately I have been using the chawanmushi cups to make Brazilian pudim. The last time I made pastel, I tried it with cheese and omochi. Using omochi in this way reminded me that some California company makes pizza omochi, garlic-cheese omochi, and raisin-cinnamon omochi. Another company specializes in jalapeño and smoked tofu. The other day we received a fancy box of chocolate-covered rice crackers. In Japan, McDonald's has a teriyaki-chicken burger, the pizzas all have corn on them, and curry rice comes with pickled ginger. A Hawaiian outfit sells popcorn mix that adds furikake[4] and rice crackers with the butter to the final product. I heard some Brazilian women have used the rice cooker to bake cakes. Nothing is sacred. Your tradition is someone else's originality. It's a big taste adventure. And then again, "Raisu, hitotsu." Gochisosamadeshita.[5]

---

[3] a gift, souvenir   [4] a rice seasoning with seaweed flakes, sesame seeds, shaved bonito, etc.   [5] literally, I have received a feast. Spoken at the close of a meal to thank the host

Hantai

国

JOSÉ RAN HOME. HE DIDN'T WANT HER TO SEE HIM CRYING, but she did. She ran after him. "José! José!" Iara called. "You're going the wrong way!" He was so unhappy and confused, he was running down the wrong street. Soon he would be lost. All the streets looked the same, and he couldn't read the signs. She kept following him, losing him from time to time behind a bicycle or a car. Finally he stopped running. He must have realized his mistake. "What are you following me for?" he yelled at her. "Go away, you stupid Japanese girl!"

"I'm not a stupid Japanese girl!" Iara yelled back.

He looked at her in surprise. He had never heard her speak Portuguese.

"What? You speak Portuguese?"

"Of course," she said. Then she admitted, "I didn't before, but now that I study with Tia Célia in the afternoons, I'm getting better."

"What do you mean?"

"I'm Brazilian like you, but I came here when I was just two years old. I never spoke Portuguese until a little while ago."

"What are we doing here?" he cried. "I hate it here. I want to go home."

"If you want to go home, it's not this way," she said. "It's that way," she pointed.

"That's not my home."

"Come on," Iara said, and José followed her sadly.

He followed her through the maze of narrow streets, hopping over the open gutters, waiting for cars backing into alleys and driveways, checking for cars around corners. She stopped before a corrugated steel sliding door that pulled down to conceal a storefront. "How did you know where I live?" he asked.

"I saw you when you arrived the other day. You don't remember? I was here helping my mother make pastéis. She uses Tia Alice's kitchen on the weekends. I saw you move in upstairs."

"Oh," he nodded. "Where are you going?"

"To Tia Célia's to study Portuguese. Want to come?"

"Can't you see I already know Portuguese?"

"Do you know everything?"

"I would if I could stay in Brazil."

Iara thought about this.

José's face struggled with his tears. Suddenly he ran behind the storefront and up the back stairs.

Iara turned to see Alice and her husband Joji arriving in their van. They had finished their deliveries and shopping for the day. They were unloading sacks of rice, beans, frozen meats, and pasta from the van. They also had Styrofoam containers used for packaging the obentos. Joji pushed up the sliding door to open the storefront. "Oh, Ia-chan," he spoke in Japanese. "What are you doing here?"

"I came with José," she answered in Japanese. "He was going the wrong way."

"Wrong way?"

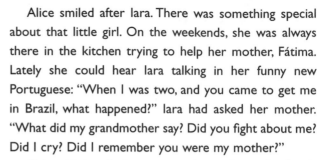

"It wasn't his fault. You can't see when you are crying. He got mixed up."

"Crying? Why crying?"

"He misses Brazil, but maybe the children were teasing him."

Alice was marching back and forth with packages. "What's the matter?" she asked.

"It's José," Joji said. "Coitado," he added in Portuguese.

"I'm late for my Portuguese class," Iara remembered. "I'd better go." She ran off before Alice could question her.

Alice smiled after Iara. There was something special about that little girl. On the weekends, she was always there in the kitchen trying to help her mother, Fátima. Lately she could hear Iara talking in her funny new Portuguese: "When I was two, and you came to get me in Brazil, what happened?" Iara had asked her mother. "What did my grandmother say? Did you fight about me? Did I cry? Did I remember you were my mother?"

Fátima bit her lip but continued to roll out the dough for the pastéis. "It was the most beautiful thing, you know, Iara. I was so worried that you had forgotten me. I brought all these presents thinking I would even bribe you to my side, but when I arrived home after all those months, you opened your little arms and ran to hug me. That's when I knew we had to be together no matter what."

Iara hugged her mother's waist. "It's a good thing I came too. Else how could you make such good pastéis, né, mamãe?"

"Come on. We'd better hurry. We have a lot more to make." Fátima wiped her eyes. "Now that you can speak Portuguese, you are full of questions. Why is that?"

"Tia Célia says it's good to ask questions to find out things. We practice asking questions all the time."

Alice thought about how speaking Portuguese had changed the relationship between Fátima and her daughter. It was as if they were trying to make up for lost time, for all the time Fátima spent working away from Iara.

Alice thought back to when she first met Fátima while working in the hospital. It was June. She remembered the month because it was beginning to get hot and muggy, and Fátima couldn't get used to the weather at all. She came from a town in Paraná, Londrina. It was hot there, she said,

but not like this and not in June, which is winter in Brazil.

The two of them were nurse's aides. They made good money in those days, as much as 6,000 dollars a month, plus they lived in the hospital and had practically no living expenses. They were working or on call twenty-four hours a day with every other weekend off, but in the summer they felt slightly lucky at having the benefit of air conditioning in the hospital.

Alice made Fátima leave the hospital on her days off to explore Japan. They usually went shopping to find clothing or toys for Iara. Alice remembered one day in particular when Fátima started to bawl in the middle of Tokyu Hands. Fátima suddenly realized she couldn't really know Iara's size, that she was missing out on her growing. She had already missed her first steps, her first words. She was making a lot of money and sending it all home to her mother to care for Iara. As a single parent, it seemed to be the right thing to do at the time, but after several months, Fátima was sick with remorse over leav-

ing Iara behind. Before the end of the year, she was on a plane home to get her.

With Iara in Japan, though, it hadn't been easy. Fátima couldn't make the big money she had been making by working at the hospital all day and all night. She had to be home, or she had to pay for child care. And she had to do it all by herself. Alice helped out when she could, by marketing Fátima's frozen pastéis on the side and letting her use her kitchen every weekend.

The years passed. But it seemed like they had arrived just yesterday, and that Iara was still a tiny toddler.

It was Alice's idea that Iara learn Portuguese. Célia needed students, but Alice also liked Célia's gentle way. She thought Iara could use that kind of attention and care, but she never imagined how much it would finally mean to Fátima.

Iara ran up the four flights of concrete stairs in building number five. Célia lived in a big housing complex called a danchi. Her apartment building was one of ten buildings, all alike, forty apartments to a build-

ing, balconies hung with bedding and drying clothing. Iara pushed her shoes off with her heels, leaving them in the genkan, and slid into the small living room. All of the apartments were the same, but every occupant had a slightly different

89

arrangement of furniture. Célia had covered the tatami with a carpet and squeezed a small sofa, a dining table with four chairs, and a cabinet with books and school  materials into the tiny room. She had a chart with the alphabet and a small blackboard on the wall. On the sliding paper doors she had pasted colorful green and yellow Brazilian posters. Lúcio and Asako were already at the table, busy writing in their workbooks.

"I'm late because I had to help a friend," Iara apologized. "He just got here from Brazil, and he was going to get lost. He was going hantai."

Célia smiled. "Good for you." She paused. "You mean your friend was going in the opposite direction. Is that what you mean?"

"Opposite direction," Iara repeated and corrected herself. She pulled a workbook from her backpack. "I'm going to finish my book today, Tia. I only have five more pages."

"I have the next workbook saved just for you." Célia pointed to a new book on the table.

"I don't have any money today, but can I still start my new book?" Iara looked concerned. "My mother says she can pay you next week. We promise. I'm going to help sell twice as many pastéis this weekend, don't you know, Tia?"

"I know, Iara. Don't worry. This book has your name on it."

Lúcio looked up from his work. "Why is Iara going so fast? She started after me, and now she's already on book five."

"We each have our own pace," Célia patted Lúcio on the shoulder. "You have to listen to your own rhythm."

"Besides," argued Iara, "I have more to catch up on than you. Look at my size. I'm nine already. If I'm going to get my diploma, I have to catch up."

"Calm down," Célia motioned. "Everyone is doing just fine. But let's get to work."

Iara had started taking classes only six months prior, and Célia was amazed at her progress and determination. Most children raised and educated in Japanese schools since early childhood spoke only Japanese. They were embarrassed to speak Portuguese with their parents or in public. Some children could translate back and forth between languages, but many children might understand  some Portuguese but only speak in Japanese. When they came to Célia, some were terribly shy; others were stubbornly resistant to or afraid of speaking any Portuguese. She worked patiently with each child. Her place was a haven for mistakes and encouragement.

One Brazilian mother had come to Célia and wept about her little boy, showing her a letter from the school which had been translated into Portuguese for her benefit. The letter explained that her son was very troubled because he did not understand his mother's language and could not communicate at home. He had told his teacher that he hated his parents because they worked until late every night. He rarely saw or spoke with them, and when he spoke in Japanese—the only language he now understood—  his parents did not understand him. Célia had promised to help the boy, but he suddenly disappeared with his mother. She later heard that the parents had separated, and the mother had gone on to another city and another job.

That was two years ago, before Célia even imagined having a school in her small six-mat living room. For weeks, Célia dreamed about the boy and his mother. She also worried about her own children, a boy and girl. Would they face each other one day and find themselves unable to speak a common language? She had seen a newspaper article about an educator who had developed a long-distance correspondence course for Brazilian students in Japan. Students could study on their own by following a series of workbooks, sending their work in for correction and comments. Ideally, they could gather periodically at centers with trained teachers to have their work examined and to get additional tutoring. After a few phone calls, Célia signed on to start a teaching center. Her first students were her own children.

"Tia," Iara announced, "I have a good subject to write about today. I want to write about my new friend José. They are teasing him in school the same way they used to tease me. His name is José, so they were making fun calling him josei, josei, like that, like he was a girl."

"I know how you got teased, Iara," Lúcio offered. "Yara yara yara!" he taunted in Japanese making a face and waving his hands.

Célia looked confused.

"He's right, Tia," Iara nodded sadly. "My name in Japanese means something like awful or stinky or ugly."

"Your name isn't Japanese. Iara is a beautiful Indian name," Célia reassured her.

Asako had been diligently at work but interrupted to add, "You think your name is bad, what about my name: saco! Que saco![1] At least no one here in Japan makes fun of my name."

"The whole world needs lessons in respect," suggested Célia. "How old is your friend?" she asked Iara.

"He's in my class, so he must be nine, too."

Célia nodded. He would be speaking Japanese in no time, but it would be difficult to catch up with the other children. The Japanese school system would simply graduate him to the next grade according to his age whether he knew his kanji or was reading at his grade level or not.

[1] sack or bag; to be fed up, "what a drag!"

If he did not study hard, he might be left behind. Still, he was luckier than some other children Célia knew who arrived in Japan at thirteen or fourteen.

"I got here when I was nine," offered Asako, "and I'm doing okay, but if you're like my brother, who was fourteen, you can't catch up ever. He was completely out of it, so he started hanging out at the pinball place and getting into trouble. My father said, if he was going to do that, he might as well work. So they faked his age, and he's making a lot of money in the factory. But he hates it. That's why I'm going to get my diploma and go to a university. If I can't get in in Japan, I'm going to go to Brazil."

"Me too," nodded Iara.

Célia knew some kids who were making hundreds of dollars a week. They bought expensive motorcycles and raced them around the neighborhood. It might be fun for a while, but they had lost their opportunity for an education both in Japan and in Brazil. The only thing left to do would be to work in the factories at repetitive jobs. She wanted to save these children, but at the same time, she knew her own husband had a university degree and had worked in a bank in São Paulo. Now they depended on his job pressing parts for Toyota cars. Saving these children was more complicated than just helping them get a diploma.

When Iara arrived home in the evening, her mother was already there. Usually Iara got to the apartment before her mother got home from the factory. She'd help start dinner by washing the rice. But that evening Iara noticed two pairs of strange shoes—men's shoes—in the doorway. She heard the men toasting with their beers before she saw them sitting on the tatami around the small table. Her mother was smiling happily. She had already changed out of her factory clothing and pulled the scarf from her hair. They were seated around the small table drinking and crunching on rice crackers. Fátima had also fried a pile of pastéis. Iara could immediately tell that one man was a Brazilian nisei like her mother, but the other was what Alice liked to call her husband: a mattaku[2] Japanese. The men were talking business, making calculations on pieces of paper. There was a lot of happy excitement, but what Iara

---

[2] literally, entirely, completely; in this case, bona fide

noticed was that from time to time, the nisei held her mother's hand and kissed her cheek.

"Fátima tells me that you are in the same class as José," the nisei tried to open a conversation with Iara.

"José? You mean José who lives upstairs from Tia Alice's kitchen?"

"That's right. He's my nephew. His dad Sérgio is my brother."

"José's angry. He doesn't want to be in Japan. He wants to go home to Brazil."

"Just like his dad." He nodded significantly at Fátima as if she should know. "They were living in Inuyama, but the empreiteira there was taking too big of a cut. Now that they're here near us, things should get better. José has to be patient. You'll be his friend, won't you?" Then he spoke in Japanese, so that the mattaku Japanese could hear. "Teach him Japanese. There are plenty of opportunities in Japan as long as you keep learning and keep an open mind. Isn't that right, Marukami-san?"

Marukami smiled and grunted and poured another round of beer. He and Mário were making plans to start their own empreiteira company. Mário had the money he'd saved over the years plus the contacts among Brazilians. Marukami would help with the Japanese documents and bureaucracy and meet with the Japanese companies looking to hire workers. They had just bought a company car and were about to lease a block of apartments for housing. They were full of big plans.

Fátima looked on at her daughter, hoping that Iara and Mário would get along. She almost wanted the two men to leave so that she could ask Iara what she thought. If Iara didn't like Mário, then she would have to think again about their relationship. But if Iara could think of Mário as a friend and maybe even as a father, per-  haps things would change. Perhaps life would be easier with a partner to share the work. But it wasn't just the work, of course; he was kind and giving, and they were slowly falling in love. She had met him at the factory. He was one of the few nisei who had risen to manager. He wasn't like the others, she thought. He was a go-getter, always looking for opportunities, full of optimism and assurance. Just being around Mário made Fátima feel hopeful and energetic.

In the middle of the festivities, Mário's cellphone rang. He pulled it from his pocket and flipped it open. Fátima got up to fry more pastéis, while Iara listened intently to Mário's side of the conversation.

"Where did he go? Where is he now? Are you all right? I'll be right there. Stay calm. I'll be there in a few minutes. How about José? Is he all right? Okay. Okay. Tchau."

Mário got up and walked to Fátima's side in the kitchen. "I've got to go. My brother Sérgio and his wife got in a fight. He's drunk again. He gets like this. He used to disappear for days and then show up looking foolish. But where's he going to disappear to in Japan?"

Marukami-san, too, got up, apologized, and left with Mário.

Iara watched the men wobble into their shoes and close the door behind them. She turned to her mother. "It's José's father isn't it, mamãe?"

Fátima nodded.

The phone rang. This time it was Alice. Fátima sighed into the phone. "I'll be there earlier tomorrow to help clean up. Don't worry. Daijobu."[3] When she hung up, she looked tired. "Iara, we have to go earlier than usual to Alice's kitchen tomorrow. She says everything in the kitchen is turned over, and some things might be broken."

"Why, mamãe?"

"José's father must have gone crazy, I guess."

The next day Iara followed her mother, crouching under the sliding door and into Alice's kitchen to survey the mess. José's mother was shoveling flour from the floor with a dustpan, which she then dumped into a trash can. White clouds burst from the can, and the dust settled into what Iara realized were pools of cooking oil. Alice came out from behind the freezer with buckets and rags. "Watch where you step," she warned.

José's mother looked up. She looked miserable. Her eyes were red and puffy. She sniffled back tears. "I'm so ashamed," she whispered to no one in particular.

Alice marched over and handed Fátima the buckets and rags. Then she put her arms around José's mother. "Listen, Yoshiko, it's just stuff. Food. Utensils. And things turned upside down. But we can put it all upright again. Nothing is broken, not even the rice cookers. Just dented. At least you weren't hurt."

"He never hurts me," Yoshiko sobbed. "He's never touched me. He only destroys everything in sight. I'm always cleaning up after him." She turned over a drawer

of spilled utensils. "But this was not his to destroy. How could he do this after everything you've done for us? I'm so ashamed," she repeated, and wept.

Alice grunted, "Just like my ex-husband. He was an alcoholic too. Made a mess and came back like a pussycat. Finally, I said no."

Fátima stepped toward the sobbing woman and patted her on the back.

"I'm so sorry," she apologized to Fátima. "The kitchen should have been ready for you to use today. I was cleaning up last night when he came in and—"

Alice interrupted, "If we can clean this area here and this counter, Fátima can start her work on time. We can just keep cleaning around her while she works." Alice

---

[3] "It's all right."

smiled at Iara who seemed stunned by everything she saw and heard. "Isn't that right, Iara?"

For some reason the women seemed to rally their resources when they heard Iara's name. They had to show her what they were made of. They couldn't sink into that paste of flour and oil and who-knew-what-else,  sliding around in a big goop on the kitchen floor. Fátima started picking up the large cans of tomato paste and replacing them on the shelves. José's mother continued her battle with the mounds of dumped flour.

"Maybe this is a sign," thought Alice out loud. "I've been thinking about quitting the obento business. Joji and I need to stop driving all over to make deliveries. We want to turn this place into what they call an internet cafe."

"What?" Fátima asked.

"Start a restaurant with computers in it."

"You're crazy," Fátima groaned and laughed at the same time. "When will you ever stop?"

"Never." Alice grinned.

Iara picked up overturned chairs and wondered about José. "Tia," she asked José's mother, "is José upstairs?"

His mother nodded. "Do you want to see him? Why don't you go on up?" she urged.

Iara ran around and up the steps. José was sitting in

front of the television. It was *Doraemon*, a Japanese cartoon. Even though he did not understand the words, he still stared. Doraemon was big and round, happy and friendly. Maybe José didn't know what had happened to his father, or that his mother was crying downstairs. Iara couldn't tell. Maybe he was just pretending that nothing had happened at all, the way Iara pretended that what her mother said was true, that her father had died before she was born.

Downstairs, the three women worked side by side.

At one point, Alice flipped open her cellphone and dialed a hotline for Brazilians with problems. After a lengthy conversation, she shared her information. "I talked to the psychologist. She says you have to get your husband himself to call. It can't be through a third party. She gets calls like this all the time, but the individual has to ask for help. But even if he calls, she can only talk over the phone. She's not licensed to work in Japan, so he's got to see a Japanese doctor, but so far there are none who speak Portuguese. She's suggesting that he go home to get help.  The problem is that a lot of people come to Japan thinking they can run away from their problems. Coming to Japan just makes it worse."

Fátima and Yoshiko nodded in agreement.

"I thought things would be better for us, especially if

he could make some good money," Yoshiko said sadly.

"Why are the brothers so different?" asked Fátima. "I mean, Mário is so positive, full of ideas and plans. He knows exactly what he wants, and he doesn't have illusions about hard work in Japan."

"I didn't know you knew Mário." Alice was surprised.

"We met at work. I guess we're dating," Fátima admitted.

Alice and Yoshiko exchanged looks. They worked quietly, saying nothing for a long while. Then Alice spoke up. "You know, Fátima, Mário is married. He has a wife and child back in Brazil."

Yoshiko paused for a moment and said, "It's not like that, Fátima. Mário is a good man. He always helps me when his brother goes on a rampage. He helped to get us here. And  in five years, he's never failed to send money to his wife and child. He told me about you, well, about a woman he likes, but I didn't know it was you. He told me that he's never felt this way. I didn't know what to tell him. It's been lonely for him, I guess."

Fátima nodded.

Yoshiko knew Mário's wife, who was not nisei like Fátima. She was a morena[4] with curly hair. Mário's parents never really liked her. They wanted him to marry a Japanese, but he always did what he wanted. That was the way he was. It was Sérgio, his brother, who always did what his parents wanted but who never really knew what he himself wanted.

Suddenly Iara popped through the door. "José's father is back," she announced. She pointed upstairs. "He came in and went to bed," she added.

Fátima looked up and smiled with relief. The commotion that churned in her stomach over this new information about Mário settled with the sight of her daughter. Then she saw the corrugated door inch up, sunlight flooding the dusty air behind Iara. Mário stood in the doorway, smiling back.

On the following Monday, Iara saw Joji standing outside the schoolyard at the end of the day. He was reading a magazine, peeking over it from time to time. She knew Joji had three of his own children, but they went to another school. What could he be doing here?

Joji thought about the mother of his children and how he had come home one day and discovered that she was gone. They were four, six, and eight at the time. What was he supposed to feed them? Suddenly he had to care for them on his own. He woke up at four in the morning to prepare meals, to wash and clean and iron, and to get them to school before he left for work. Sometimes he skipped out of work to see teachers and always rushed

[4] brunette

home in the evenings to make dinner and help with homework. He was exhausted. Often they were left on their own. Neighbors watched them, told them to stay out of the streets. One day he visited a friend in the hospital. The nurse's aide caring for his friend was a Brazilian nisei named Alice.

Alice had already raised her children, now grown, in Brazil. At age forty, she had come alone to Japan for a change, to start a new life. She never imagined that a new life might mean raising another family and starting her own business. Joji watched her reorganize his family, put his children to work to care for each other, and start her obento business for Brazilians. Her energy and exuberance filled their lives. Plain rice was exchanged for the Brazilian taste of garlic, salt, and olive oil with a ladle of beans. The dark cloud of his wife's disappearance lifted. He quit his job and went into the obento business, too. Now he and Alice worked side by side day after day. He did the driving, shopping, deliveries, and much of the negotiating. She was still learning Japanese, and he was picking up Portuguese here and there. Sometimes they fought over misunderstandings, but laughed about it later.

Over his magazine, he could see Fátima's little girl, Iara, waiting at the other end of the schoolyard. Iara was like Alice, he decided. Happy like Alice. He often puzzled over his new wife, this nisei, so filled with life and love for

KAREN TEI YAMASHITA

his children. Was it Brazil? he wondered. He could not have gone to Brazil, but Brazil had miraculously come to him. He knew there was something to learn from this, something to give back for this blessing.

Iara had decided to stay behind to watch out for José. She wanted to follow him home again to make sure he didn't get lost. She saw José leaving school, a small crowd of boys following him and laughing. Joji spotted José too and followed the boys down the street. He called to José, urging him in Portuguese, "Go home. Go home, José. It's okay." Suddenly, Joji cornered the boys. One got away, but the others had to stay and listen to Joji's tirade. Iara could hear him yelling at them. "Who do you think you are?" he yelled. "Teasing this lonely boy who has never done anything to any of you! You don't even know his name or where he's come from or what he likes to do or why he is here. You are all too foolish to even find out or care. You could be his friend, but instead you make him an outsider. You should be ashamed of yourselves. Look into your hearts and think about your actions. Who taught you to treat another human being so cruelly?"

Iara was surprised to see Joji so angry. She had never seen him like this. It was really amazing. She wanted to cheer and jump up and down. Finally someone had come to save José and her. As the boys left, ashamed, she ran up to Joji and hugged him fiercely.

政

日本のルール

1. 家や建物に入るときには靴を脱ぐ。
2. 人を訪ねるときには、必ずオミヤゲをもってゆく。
3. お箸をご飯茶碗に二本の柱のように突き立てたままにしない。
4. ４という数字は避けなさい。
5. 自分の年齢と季節に見合った格好をすること。
6. おなじ仕事をしても、男には時給千二百円、女には時給九百円を払うべし。
7. トイレではスリッパを使いなさい。そしてそれをトイレに脱いでくるのを忘れない。
8. 主の側に強いられるまでは、すべてエンリョすること。
9. お風呂ではお湯につかる前に浴槽の外で体を洗うこと。
   そしてタオルはお湯につけてはいけません。
10. 車は左側通行。道が狭すぎるときには、真ん中を走りなさい。
11. キモノを着るときは、左側を前にする。
12. 昇給と昇進に関しては、一覧表になった年齢別の規定にしたがうこと。
13. 彼の意見は彼女の意見は私の意見はあなたの意見。はい、賛成でーす。

ルール看板
（ホミ団地にあった日本語とポルトガル語併記の大きな看板。同団地は愛知県豊田市保見ケ丘にあり、
およそ八千人が住んでいて、うち二千人がブラジル人だ。）

団地の決まりを守りましょう！
－許可証なく駐車しないでください。

－オートバイのスピードの出しすぎはやめましょう。

－深夜や夜明け前に広場を使うのはやめましょう。

－道路や建物のまわりに缶や瓶を投げ捨てるのはやめましょう。

－壁や設備に落書きするのはやめましょう。

－アパートでのパーティーや集会では、騒音に気をつけてください。

－ベランダでのバーベキューはやめましょう。

－騒音公害に気をつけましょう。

－テレビやステレオの音は控えめに。

－大声で話をすると、ご近所の迷惑になります。

－ゴミは決まったやり方で決まった場所に出しましょう。

－アパートの窓からゴミや物を投げないでください。

－特に煙草のポイ投げが多いようです。吸殻を投げないでください。

団地はみんなが楽しく暮らすところです。
ご近所の人たちのことも考えて、毎日気持ち良く暮らせるようにしましょう。

中部住宅供給公団名古屋事務所

ルール看板の他に、ホミ団地ではチラシが配られ、以下の規則がポルトガル語で説明してある。

毎日の暮らしのための注意

① 当公団住宅にはさまざまな人が住んでいて、みなそれぞれ生活のリズムがちがいます。それに日本の文化と習慣は、他の国のそれとはちがいます。全員が公共生活の規則を守り、ご近所の方とのあいだに問題が生じるのを避けるようお願いします。

② ラジオやテレビの音を大きくするのは、特に早朝と深夜には、やめてください。早朝深夜には廊下でも、自分の部屋でも、騒音を立てないようにしましょう。

③ アパートで猫や犬その他の動物を飼うことは、ご近所の迷惑になるかもしれないので禁止されています。

④ ゴミは各戸ごとに仕分けなくてはなりません。ゴミは決まった曜日に決まった場所に出しましょう。前の晩や、その他、規定外の時間に出すのは禁止されています。野良犬やその他の動物が夜間にゴミをまき散らして住民やご近所の迷惑になることがあるからです。

⑤ 入居者組合の活動は、毎月住民が組合におさめる活動費によって実行されます。組合の毎月の収入は、催し物やお知らせの印刷、備品購入、結婚のお祝いや御香典など、全般の運営費用として使われます。組合費はまた、団地に日々不可欠な諸経費、たとえば階段や廊下や通路やホールや集会室の光熱費、諸設備の維持修繕、空き地の整備、配管や下水、共用水道などにも使われます。組合費の納入が遅れると組合の活動も遅れ、結局は住民自身の不便となります。毎月の入居者組合費は、家賃とおなじくきちんと納めるようにしましょう。

⑥ 入居者組合ならびに市からのお知らせは、回覧板で通知されます。お知らせを読んだらただちに、回覧板を次のお宅にまわしてください。

⑦ 入居者組合ではときどき共同清掃や草むしりをします。共同清掃は住民の仕事ですので、みなさんのご協力をお願いいたします。

またお祭りやその他の親睦の集いもあります。ぜひ参加して、他の住民との交流を深めるようにしてください。

ブラジル人には、こうしたルールのすべてにしたがうことは、むずかしかった。大きな音で音楽をかけてはだめ。広場で深夜おしゃべりをしてはいけません。シュラスコ（ブラジル風バーベキュー）はご遠慮ください。単車で走りまわらないこと。おまけにゴミは、決まった日の決まった時間に決まった手順で決まった場所に、非常に細かく仕分けて出さなくてはならない（燃えるもの、缶、瓶、壊れもの、粗大ゴミ）。ブラジル人は回覧板をまわすのを忘れたり、その内容を読まなかったりした。さて、共同清掃の日は毎月いちど、日曜の朝8時半からと決まっている。ご近所の日本人たちが植え込みを刈ったり、道を掃いたり、草をむしったりしているあいだ、ブラジル人たちはベッドで寝返りを打っていた。日曜日の、こんなとんでもない時間に起きだすよりは、罰金を払ったほうがましだったのだ。

　そうこうしているうちに、日本人の住民は、もう我慢ならなくなった。ブラジル人はルールを守らない。かれらがいるおかげで、整然とした生活がめちゃめちゃになってしまった。この団地に住んでいるのでなければ、この不満を想像することはむずかしい。ホミ団地とその周辺を実際に歩いてみると、そこには重苦しい無音がのしかかっていることがわかる。夜勤の人たちが眠っている音、なんとか受け入れられたいと願っている沈黙する多数派の音、必死になってしずかにしようとしている人々の音。子供たちまで、しずかに遊んでいるようだ。これはブラジル人としては可能なかぎりのしずけさだ。おそらくブラジル人にとっては、これが最高にルールを守っている状態なのだ。

ブラジルのルール

1. ルールというものはない。
2. すべてのルールは破ることも回避することもできる。
3. ダール・ウン・ジェイチーニョ。（何事にも必ず抜け道があるもの。）
4. パーティーにはいつでも赤ん坊や子供を連れてゆくこと。
5. 男はベランダでビール。女は台所に集まる。
6. パーティーでおいとまするときには、たっぷり一時間ばかりかけて全員にキスをしたり抱きしめたりすること。
7. 女性どうし。キス二つなら、ただの挨拶。キス三つは、結婚のしるし。キス四つは、義母と一緒に暮らすのを避けるため。
8. 男性どうし。左手は相手の肩に。右手でおなかをぽんぽんと叩く。
9. 神聖不可侵なものは何もない。ジョークのネタにせよ。
10. ある状況を巧く利用したからって、別に盗んだことにはならない。
11. 何をやってもうまくゆかないのだから、何もしないことが最善策かも。

ブラジル人は、非常に肉体派だ。お互いによくさわりあう。キスし、抱擁する。会ったらキスし、抱擁し、別れるときにもまたキスし、抱擁する。頬がほんのちょっと、ちょうどいいだけ接触するように他人に顔を近づけるのは、身につけるまでに一苦労する技だ。それはまったく自然で友好的に見えるけれど、この接触にはちゃんとしたルールがあるのだ。ある日本人の男はすっかり興奮して、あるブラジル女性の乳房をわしづかみにしてしまった。彼女は鉄パイプをもちだし、もう少しで彼をめった打ちにするところだった。のちに男は、たしかにやりすぎだったがどうしようもなかったのだ、といった。あのおっぱいが、信じられないくらい美しすぎたからだと。

それでもブラジル人は、「抱擁」（アブラッソ）に関して、はっきりした考えをもっている。手紙を書くときには、抱擁を送る。「口づけ」（ベイジョ）を送る。ブラジル人が期待するのは、こうして愛情をしめすのが、心の温かさや気さくさの表現となるということだ。これがなければ、世界とは冷たい場所になってしまう。だから、こうしたキスに面食らってしまう文化の人々は、冷たい人々だということになる。フリオ（冷たい）なのだ。アメリカ人や日本人は、人前で愛情をしめすことがほとんどない。単なる知人にキスをすることは、ちょっとゆきすぎだと思われる。握手だけで十分。それとも、ちょっとお辞儀するとか。それはおそらく冷たい温かいの問題ではない。どうするのが、体に気持ちいいかということなのだろう。ブラジル人はキスする。日本人は、一緒に裸になってお風呂に入る。

二世／三世にとってのよく知られた心的外傷のひとつに、両親がお互いに、あるいは子供に、接触による愛情を表現しないということがある。そうした愛情表現の欠落は、ブラジル社会において、あるいはアメリカ社会においてですら、日系の子供たちにはアイデンティティ危機の原因となりうる。たとえば「私は両親が私を愛していないのだと思った」というように。私自身の家族の、一方の家系はよそよそしいタイプ、もう一方の家系ははぐはぐべたべたというタイプだったので、私は愛情にはいろいろな表現があるのだということを学ばなくてはならなかった。それでも日本人どうしは握手すらしないということを見ながら育ってきた私は、どうやら日本人は肉体的接触を完全に避けるのだと、思いこんでいたようだ。私の戯曲のひとつを上演するのに日本人の演出家と仕事をしたとき、私の作った日本人のキャラクターどうしに彼女が肉体的接触をさせるのを見て、ようやく私はこの考え方を捨てたのだった。

発表します。
日本人どうしも体に触れあうことはあるんです。

アブラッソス・エ・ベイジョス（抱擁と口づけ）。それはラテン系の人々のあいだでは、洗練された技法となっている。抱きしめたりキスをしたりするのは規則外のことで、ルールとはすべて私たちをお互いから遠ざけるものばかりだと考えることはたやすい。けれどもまた、抱きしめたりキスをしたりというのもそれ自体でルールなのであり、それをしなければ私たちはお互いから遠ざけられてしまうのだと考えることもできる。そういうわけで、またもや、私はあなたを遠くから抱きしめよう。それはルールを超えた、長距離抱擁だ。

103

アメリカのルール

1. 英語を話しなさい。
2. 金持ちがルールを作る。
3. 公共の場所および飛行機では禁煙。
4. ともかく、やってみる。
5. 疑わしいときには弁護士に相談せよ。
6. コークを飲もう。リアルなものを楽しもう。
7. われわれが世界。
8. わが国が、地球上でもっとも幸福な場所。
9. アメリカン・エクスプレス、
   マスターカード、ヴィザが使えます。

ずっと以前、日本人旅行者むけのこんな漫画入りパンフレットを見たことがある。外国の勝手のちがう場所で、どんな風にふるまうのが適切かという、いくつかの場面を描いたものだ。握手の仕方から、トイレの座り方（またがるのではなくて）まで、あらゆるテーマがあった。便座に足をかけてまたがるのは、床に作られた日本の便器の構造のせいだ。しゃがみこまなくてはならない。ブラジル人は、それを「モトキーニャ」（ちびバイク）という愛称で呼んだ。つまり、単車に乗るように、それに「乗る」からだ。現在では日本の公共の場所ではしばしば「洋式」と書かれた便器があり、ホテルや家庭には世界でもっとも凝ったトイレが誇らかに設置されている。

トトという会社が、暖房つきの便座、ビデ、温風乾燥システムをもったトイレを売りだしている。まったく驚くべきものだ。ビデの水の噴出口は、どういう仕組みでか、膣のほうも肛門のほうも洗えるようになっている。そう、きちんと二つの絵の表示があって、どちらかを選べるのだ。友人のお父さんが、自宅にあるそれを見せてくれて、アメリカにはこういうのはありますか、と聞いた。たぶんないでしょうね、と私がいうと、彼は冗談半分に、だったらぼくはアメリカには行けないなあ、といった。さらに、この新型トイレにして以来、トイレット・ペイパーはもう使っていないのだそうだ。私は、日本のいろんな場面での適切なふるまい方を教えてくれる漫画入りパンフレットが必要だという気になってきた。ビデのボタンを押すのはいいけど、出てくる水の温度を上げるにはどうすればいいのか？　それよりもっと緊急なのは、この水、どうやって止めればいいの？

また公共の場所のあるところでは、女性用トイレに、じつに妙な設備がある。トイレを流している音の、音響装置だ。はじめて見たとき、日本語の説明が読めないので、私はセンサーの前に何度も手をかざしては、トイレを流しつづけた。ところが奇妙なことに、ただ音が聞こえてくるだけなのだ。水は出ない。音だけ。ついに私は通訳をトイレにひっぱりこみ、説明を求めた。そうか！どうやら日本の女たちには、おしっこの音が苦になるらしい。それで放尿の音を聞こえなくするために、トイレを流しながらおしっこをする人が多い。これは水の非常なむだづかいだ。そこでトトは、音だけ出る装置を発明したのだ。登録商標です。

おまけに日本のトイレには、もっとも豪華な（大理石のカウンター、イケバナ、香水入りの石鹸などのある）ところでも、ペーパータオルが置かれていない。手を拭くには自分のハンカチをもっていなくてはならず、私はいつもそれを忘れる。その結果、トイレには紙屑の心配がない。ことによると、いつかトイレット・ペーパーもなくなるかも。トトならやりかねない。

こうした背景のもとに、ある日本人女性の心配を想像してみてほしい。彼女はブラジルに行ったり来たりすることを数年つづけたのち、はじめて、ブラジルではトイレット・ペーパーは便器の近くにある容器に捨てなくてはならなかったと気づいたのだ。世界中を旅行している彼女だが、こういうやり方は、これまで他の国ではお目にかかったことがなかった。配管のせいだろうか？　紙が水に溶けないから？　彼女は考えこんでしまった。と

んでもないまちがいを犯したように思って、謝りたかった。自分は無邪気に旅をしつつ、何十というトイレをつまらせてきたのだろうか？

ブラジルの友人、アナ・マリア・バイアーナが、『アメリカ、AからZまで』という本を書いた。この本は空港で売られていて、ブラジル人にとって度し難い、あるいは笑える、あるいは不可解、あるいは奇怪に思われる、アメリカ生活の種々の習慣や場面のことが、細かく論じられている。「B」の項目に、ビデがある。アメリカ合衆国にはビデがないのだ、と彼女は書く。アナ・マリアはビデをなつかしむが、はたして誰かがブラジルで実際にビデを使っていたかどうか、私は思いだせない。大概の家庭では、ビデには汚れた洗濯物がほうりこまれているのだ。女たちは、パンティーを洗うのに使う。それでも、どこの家にも必ずあるようだ。建材屋が、便器とビデをそろいで売っているからだ。これで一組なんですよ、ええ。

ブラジルでも公共の場所にはビデはない、もちろん。ところによってはトイレット・ペーパーもペーパー・タオルもない。その場合、わずかな金額でこれらの必需品を提供してくれる係の女性がいることがある。この女性は便器を磨いたり床にモップをかけたりして、トイレの清掃も担当することになっている。あなたが払うお金は、おそらく彼女の食事代。でもときには、このトイレのおばさんに上げる小銭の持ち合わせがないことがある。そんなときにはレディーズ・ルームから走って逃げださなくてはならない。おばさんが後を追ってこないようにと、祈りながら。

アメリカの女性は、はるかな昔に有料トイレを廃止している。これは当時のフェミニズムのなしとげた、大きな仕事だった。事実、あるアジア系アメリカ人女性は、この問題提起によって政治的名声を手に入れたのだ。おしっこを、無料に。だがここには、まだまだ争わなくてはならない問題がある。劇場で女性用トイレの無限につづく行列に加わるたび、たぶんこの劇場を設計したのは男だったのだということを、思い知らされずにはいられないのだから。

アメリカの公共用トイレの特徴は、大量の紙だ。巨大なトイレット・ペーパーのロールのおかげで紙がなくて困ることはないし、やがてはゴミ箱からあふれて外にこぼれ落ちることになる、ありあまるペーパー・タオルがある。何より重要なのは、アメリカのトイレにはふつう紙のシートがあるということだ。トイレでお隣にいる女性が容器から紙シートをやぶりとり、それを便座にびしゃぴしゃ押さえつけている音が聞こえる。便座には、どんな気持ち悪いものがついているか、知れたものではないのだ。「浮かせ方式」を採用する女性もいる。つまり、便座にお尻がふれないようにして腰をかがめるのだ。とはいえ、ままよとばかり、すわる以外にない人も多い。あるいは便座に足をのせてまたがっている人だって、いないとは断言できない。

こうしたトイレ作法がルールについて教えてくれることは、たぶんさほど多くはない。ローマ人は配管を発明した。配管を修理したことのある人なら、ローマ時代から何も変わってはいないといいたくなるはずだ。ヴェル

サイユ宮殿では、トイレというものはなかった、と聞かされる。人はただ、壁沿いのベルベットのカーテンの背後にしばし身を隠したというのだ。鹿児島の磯庭園では、着物をきたガイドが島津侯のすわったトイレを見せてくれる。殿のおなかから排出されたものは、香り高い檜の葉をしきつめた上に落下したという。そこでトイレをのぞきこめば、たしかにいまも、檜の葉が枝ごとしかれている。ルールのうち、あるものは儀礼。そしてあるものは単なる習慣にすぎない。

サークルKのルール

1. 自分の祖国に移民せよ。
2. 好きな料理は自分で作れるようにする。
3. つねに、その次の問い、を問うこと。

政

Japanese Rules

1. Remove your shoes when entering houses and buildings.
2. Always bring omiyage[1] when you visit as a guest.
3. Don't leave your chopsticks stuck in your rice bowl like two posts.
4. Avoid the number four.
5. Dress according to your age and the season.
6. For the same work: Pay men 1,200 yen per hour; pay women 900 yen per hour.
7. Use the toilet slippers, but don't forget to leave them with the toilet.
8. Enryo[2] until your host insists.
9. Wash outside the bath before soaking, and don't bring the towel in with you.
10. Drive on the left side of the road; if it's too narrow, drive in the middle.
11. When wearing a kimono, wrap yourself left over right.
12. Follow the table for incremental salary increases and title changes according to a man's age.
13. His opinion is her opinion is my opinion is your opinion. I agree.

[1] gift   [2] to hesitate, show reserve, stand on ceremony

The Rule Board

(A large sign written in both Japanese and Portuguese at Homi-Danchi, a condominium complex housing some 8,000 people—2,000 of whom are Brazilian—in Homi-gaoka, Toyota City)

Let's respect the rules of the residential condominium!

Please do not park without requesting permission.

Let's stop driving motorcycles at high speeds.

Please don't use the plaza late at night and before the sun rises.

Let's stop throwing cans and bottles in the streets and around the buildings.

Please don't write on the walls or objects.

During parties or reunions in apartments, please take care with the noise.

* Let's stop barbecuing on the verandah.

Let's take care with noise pollution.

* Please regulate the volume on your television and stereo system.

* Conversing in loud voices bothers your neighbors.

Please put trash out in accordance with the determined models and in the appropriate location.

Do not throw objects or trash out of apartment windows.

* In particular, the throwing of cigarettes is common; please do not throw them.

 The residential condominium is a place where many people live communally. Let's collaborate to have a pleasurable daily life, thinking also of our neighbors.

—Municipal Corporation for Habitational Conservation
Chubu Branch / Nagoya Office

In addition to the Rules Board, flyers are also distributed throughout Homi-Danchi explaining the following regulations in Portuguese:

Precautionary Notice for Daily Living

① *In these public housing units live various people, each with a different rhythm of life. Furthermore, the culture and customs of Japan are different from that of other countries. Thus, we ask that each person respect the regulations of communal life, to avoid any problems with your neighbors.*

② *Do not turn on radios and televisions at high volume, principally in the early morning and late hours at night. Also during this time, take care not to make noise in the corridors or even in your apartment.*

③ *It is prohibited to raise cats, dogs, or any other animal in the apartment because this may cause inconveniences for your neighbors.*

④ *In each home, the trash must be separated by category. This trash should be left in specific locations on specific days of the week. It is prohibited to throw trash out on the previous night or at other inappropriate times. Stray dogs and other animals can spread the trash during the night, causing inconvenience to the residents and neighbors.*

⑤ *The activities of the Association are realized through the financial resources given monthly by residents to the Residential Condominium Association. These monthly revenues are used for the operational costs of the Association, such as the realization of events, printing of bulletins, acquisition of equipment, celebratory notices and condolences, etc.*

Condominium dues serve to cover the costs of indispensable services for the daily activities of the condominium, such as the cost of electricity to illuminate stairs, corridors, passages, halls, and rooms for reunions; maintenance and repairs of installations; cleaning the land; piping and drainage; and water for collective use, etc.

Any late payments will cause delays in the operation of the Association and this will cause, in the last analysis, inconveniences to the residents themselves.

Do not forget to pay your monthly Residential Condominium Association dues before the due date in the same manner as your rent.

⑥ *Notifications of the Association of Condominium Residents and the City are circulated through clipboards. As soon as you have read these notices, pass them to the next resident.*

⑦ *From time to time, the Association of Condominium Residents has a clean-up, cutting of grass and weeds, etc., in the form of a group event. This work is realized by the residents, and the cooperation of everyone is requested.*

On the other hand, there are also festivals and other events of fraternization. Try to participate to promote friendship with other residents.

☺

The Brazilians have had difficulty following all these rules. No loud music. No late-night conversations in the plaza. No churrasco. No speeding around on motorcycles. An extremely detailed categorizing of trash (burnables, cans, bottles, breakables, large items) with specific methods for disposal, specific days and times, and specific locations for specific removal. Brazilians forget to pass the clipboard or don't read the contents. Finally, the group clean-up days are monthly on Sunday mornings at 8:30 A.M. While their Japanese neighbors are outside trimming hedges, sweeping paths, and cutting grass, the Brazilians turn over in their beds, preferring to pay the fine rather than wake up on a Sunday at such an ungodly hour.

In the meantime, the Japanese residents are at their wit's end. The Brazilians are unruly. Their presence has made a muck of a tidy routine. Not living in these housing units, it's difficult to imagine. A tour of Homi-Danchi and its environs gives you a sense of an oppressive quiet—the sound of sleeping people who work the night shift, the sound of a silent majority who want very badly to be accepted, the sound of people trying very hard to be quiet. Even the children seem to play quietly. This is as quiet as Brazilians can possibly be. This is probably as *ruly* as it gets.

Brazilian Rules

1. There are no rules.

2. All rules may be broken or avoided.

3. Dar um jeitinho. (There is always a way.)

4. Always bring your babies and small children to parties.

5. Men on the verandah with beers; women in the kitchen.

6. When leaving a party, give yourself an hour to kiss or hug each person good-bye.

7. Females: Two kisses in greeting; three kisses to marry; four to avoid living with your mother-in-law.

8. Males: Left hand on his shoulder. Right hand patting his belly.

9. Nothing is sacred: tell a joke.

10. Taking advantage of a situation is not necessarily stealing.

11. Since nothing works, doing nothing may be the best approach.

110

Brazilians are a very physical people. They touch each other a lot. They kiss and hug. They kiss and hug when meeting, and kiss and hug when taking leave. It takes some practice to master getting that close to someone's face with just the right brush of the cheek. Even though it all seems so natural and friendly, there are rules about all this touching. One Japanese man got carried away and grabbed a Brazilian woman's breasts. She hauled out a metal pipe and nearly beat him to a pulp. Later he explained his impulsive excess: those breasts were just too beautiful to believe.

Still, Brazilians have an expectation about the abraço. They send embraces in their messages. They send beijos. Their expectation is that this show of affection is a demonstration of warmth and openness. Without it, the world would be a cold place; thus, cultures who find this kissing disconcerting are a cold people. Frio. Americans and Japanese hardly show affection in public; to kiss a mere acquaintance seems a little overdone. A handshake is just fine. Or how about a little bow. It's probably not about cold or hot; it's more like what's comfortable for a body to do. Brazilians kiss. Japanese get naked together in hot baths.

One of the well-known nisei / sansei traumas has been that their parents don't show physical affection for each other or their children. A lack of such affection among Nikkei in Brazilian or even American society is cause for an identity crisis as in: "I thought my parents

didn't love me." Since one side of my family is the distant sort, and the other touchy-feely, I've had to learn that affection can be defined in many different ways. Still, growing up and seeing that Japanese never even shook hands, I had some idea that they also never touched each other. Working with a Japanese director on one of my plays and seeing her put my Japanese characters in physical contact with each other finally abolished this assumption.

♥   ANNOUNCEMENT: ♥
Japanese do in fact touch each other.

Abraços e beijos. It's a fine art among the Latins. It's easy to think that the rule is *not* hugging and kissing, that rules separate us. But it's also possible to think that hugging and kissing are rules in themselves, that without them we shall be separate. And then again, I embrace you from a great distance. It's a long embrace without rules.

立入禁止
DO NOT ENTER
PROIBIDA A ENTRADA

American Rules

1. Speak English.
2. He who *has* makes the rules.
3. Smoking is prohibited in public places and on airplanes.
4. Just do it.
5. When in doubt, consult your attorney.
6. Drink Coke. Enjoy the real thing.
7. We are the world.
8. We are the happiest place on Earth.
9. We accept American Express, Mastercard, or Visa.

☺

I remember years ago seeing a pamphlet for Japanese travelers explaining with cartoons a series of possible scenarios in foreign places and the appropriate behavior. There was everything from shaking hands to sitting (not stepping up) on the toilet seats. This had to do with the nature of the Japanese toilet, which is on the floor. You have to crouch over it. The Brazilians have fondly dubbed it the "motoquinha" meaning that you "ride" it much like a motorcycle. Now public places often have stalls marked "Western Toilet," and hotels and homes boast of the most sophisticated toilets in the world.

A company named Toto sells a toilet with a heated seat, bidet, and air-drying system. Truly amazing. Somehow the nozzle for the bidet can squirt you in the vagina or the anus. Yes, there are clearly two picture signs to choose from. My friend's father demonstrated his home model and asked me if we had such toilets in America. When I said probably not, he jokingly said in that case, he probably couldn't travel there. Furthermore, since he got his new toilet, he never uses toilet paper anymore. I began to feel that I needed my own pamphlet with cartoons explaining a series of possible scenarios and appropriate behavior. If I pressed the button for bidet, how could I raise the temperature of the water? More importantly, how could I make the squirting water stop?

Then there's this odd feature in women's toilets in some public places: *the sound of flushing*. On first inspection, I was unable to read the Japanese explanation, so I kept trying to flush the toilet by passing my hand over the sensor. Curiously, all I got was the recorded sound of flushing. No water. Just the sound. Finally I dragged an interpreter into the stall for an explanation. Ah! Apparently Japanese women have found the sound of peeing offensive, so, to mask it, they flush and pee at the same time. It's an enormous waste of water, so Toto invented *the sound of flushing.*™

Finally, Japanese bathrooms, even the most luxurious (marble counters, ikebana, perfumed soap and all), never have paper towels. You're supposed to bring your own towel, and I always forget. As a result, the bathrooms are quite litter-free. Who knows? With Toto, one day they may be toilet paper-free.

Under such conditions, imagine the concern of a Japanese woman who told me that she had been traveling back and forth to Brazil for several years before she realized that she should have been throwing her toilet paper into the receptacle provided in the stall. A world traveler, she could not remember this practice in any other country she had visited. Was it the plumbing system? Didn't the paper dissolve? she wondered. She wanted to apologize as if this were a great faux pas; had she caused dozens of toilets to clog in her innocent wake?

A Brazilian friend, Ana Maria Bahiana, has written a book, *America: A to Z*, sold in airports, detailing all the habits and situations of American life that Brazilians find exasperating, funny, unexplainable, or odd. Under "B" is bidet. There are no bidets in the USA, she notes. Ana Maria misses her bidet, but I can't remember that anyone really used it in Brazil; it was usually filled with dirty laundry. Women use them to wash their panties. Nevertheless, all houses seem to have them. The construction outlets sell the toilet with a matching bidet. It's a pair.

KAREN TEI YAMASHITA

Of course public places in Brazil don't have bidets. Some don't have toilet paper or paper towels either. In that case, there might be a woman who offers you these essentials for a small fee. This woman supposedly also cleans the bathroom, scrubbing the toilets and mopping the floors. The fee you pay is probably her dinner. But every now and then, you may not have any change for the toilet lady; you've got to run out of the ladies' room and hope she doesn't come chasing after you.

American women did away with pay toilets a long time ago. This was a major act of feminism at the time. In fact, an Asian American woman rose to political fame on this platform: pee for free. Still there's ground to cover here. Queuing up in endless lines for the ladies' room in theaters always reminds you that a man was probably the architect.

The thing about American public toilets is the great amount of paper in them: gigantic toilet paper rolls so you will never be without, and paper towels that finally fill and spill over the trash receptacles. Most importantly, American toilets usually have paper seats. You can hear the women in the other stalls ripping them out of the containers and slapping them down on the seats. You never know what could be yucking up the seat of a toilet. Some women must use the hover method where you sit without touching. Heck, some people must just sit on the seat anyway. Who knows, maybe someone is stepping up and crouching.

What all this toiletry has to say about rules is probably not erudite. The Romans invented plumbing. If you've ever tried to fix the plumbing, you feel as if nothing has changed since the Romans. At Versailles, we're told, no toilets existed; you simply disappeared for a moment behind the velvet curtains along the walls. At the Iso Gardens in Kagoshima, a guide dressed in a kimono shows you the toilet where the Lord Shimazu sat, his bowel movements falling into a bed of fragrant cedar leaves. You look in the toilet and sure enough: branches of cedar leaves. Some rules are rituals. Some habits.

Circle K Rules

1. Immigrate into your own country.
2. Learn to cook your favorite meals.
3. Ask the next question.

The Tunnel

The Tunnel

IN JULY, A CLASS ACTION SUIT WAS fiLED AGAINST THE government for knowingly endangering the health of employees involved in the work of drilling tunnels. Thousands of kilometers of tunnels, woven like catacombs under Japan's mountain ranges, form a great part of the intricate and extensive pattern of the national land transportation system. Former employees complained of contracting various forms of lung disease, including cancer. Many had died; many were close to dying. All spoke of the fine dust, the poor ventilation, difficulty breathing, and the lack of proper protective gear. These workers had dynamited their way underground for distances as long as fifteen kilometers. Holding your breath while driving through a tunnel is perhaps a kind of tribute, a connection to the suffering of dead workers. As you turn blue in the face, begin to black out from lack of oxygen,

you see their ghosts, helmeted figures in blue and gray uniforms, scarves covering their faces, their eyes squinting into the distant light. The percentage of the national highway system that lies within tunnels is probably a decipherable number, a number someone has recorded somewhere, a notable number. In such an extensive system, to speak of one tunnel may seem meaningless; on the other hand, to speak of one tunnel may be to speak of all tunnels.

The bodies were found at the opening of the tunnel, each neatly folded into two separate suitcases. The enormous suitcases were placed across the road from each other, snug to the opposite walls, matching eye-teeth in a gaping mouth. Cars and trucks sped into and out of the tunnel's deep throat, oblivious to the gatekeepers. Only the tunnel's ghosts wandered forward risking the light to greet the unfortunate newcomers.

Cida

A REPORTER TELEPHONED FROM JAPAN. SHE WANTED to know what I thought about the death of my husband. I told her that my husband had been dead five years already, or so it seemed to me. This confused her until I explained that he had left for Japan five years ago and never returned. He had left me and his three-year-old son and disappeared. He never called or wrote. Wasn't that like being dead? She asked if we had any contact at all, if he sent me money to take care of the boy.

I told her I get money every month through an account in the bank. It's always the same amount. It's enough. I don't complain. I don't want to depend on his money, so I try to take care of my life here. I didn't tell her I used to cry every day. I wrote letters but had no address to send them to. Once I got a phone number from his mother, but he was never there. Finally I gave up. The boy could use a father, but it's better if he thinks he's dead. It's better that way.

Then she told me that Mário really had been killed, murdered. The police were looking for suspects, but the crime had not been solved. She apologized for having to be the one to tell me this and waited for my reaction. I thought it must be a joke and asked her how she got my phone number. How did she know how to find me? She explained that this story was her assignment, that she had been following the story for three days already since the revelation of the murders. Her investigation led her to me, logically. She didn't understand how I wasn't informed of any of this. She had only called for a statement, wondered if I knew anything about his life in Japan, anything that might help solve the mystery of his death.

I suggested that she knew more about Mário's life in Japan than I. She told me that he had been working seven days a week, first for one contractor, then another. He was involved in starting his own contracting business and had just bought a new car. He was also involved with a woman who worked with him and who was also killed.

After the conversation with the reporter, I called Mário's folks. Mário's mother answered. They already knew everything. His brother Sérgio had called two days ago. They didn't call me because Sérgio had said that he would be the one to tell me, but I never heard from him. Mário's father got on the line because his mother started to cry and couldn't stop. He told me that reporters from all over had been calling constantly. He still had to answer the phone because it might be the consulate calling with information. Then he told me that he felt ashamed that Mário had abandoned me, that even though he never approved of our getting married, he would rather see his son alive and living with me and the boy than to have suffered such a cruel death. He would never see his son again. He broke down and cried. I could hear him sobbing on the other end for a long time, and then he hung up.

I felt guilty, as if I myself had pulled the trigger. Five years ago when he left, I knew he might not return. I threatened then that if he didn't return, I'd send someone to bring him back, even if it had to be in a box. I told him that if he ever found another woman, I'd kill her and him both. I could have saved every penny he ever sent me, used his own money to hire a killer. But the Mário I knew died five years ago, so all of this became unnecessary.

116

Sérgio

THREE WOMEN REPORTERS HAVE BEEN STAKED OUT in a car outside our place for three days now. They take turns sleeping or going off to buy food at the corner Circle K. They have their cameras and tape recorders ready. One or another is always talking into her cellphone, taking notes.

We don't leave the house if we can help it. When we do, the reporters run up, try to take photos and ask questions. I don't want my boy involved in any of this. He has already suffered enough in this country. I tell those reporters we can't talk to anyone but the police until the case is resolved. Alice left her cellphone with us. We call her or she calls us asking if we need anything. Even if she's downstairs cooking, we talk to each other by cellphone.

It feels as if every Brazilian in the town and anyone who ever knew a Brazilian has been interrogated by the police. All the workers and managers in the factory where Mário and Fátima worked have been questioned. All the neighbors and even clients who bought pastéis from Fátima as well.

Alice already talked to them and told them everything she knew. She was like a sister to Fátima. At first she was inconsolable, but she had to feed all those workers with her box lunches. She went back out there with Joji to distribute her lunches and came back angry instead. She found out that some Brazilians in town had lost their jobs, and others had their rental agreements ter-minated. Brazilians were being told that it was too risky to hire us or to rent us housing. Alice said we were being punished for being the victims of a heinous crime. Plus a lot of Brazilians were saying that this might be a hate crime against Brazilians; who knew who might be the next victim? The next time the police called her in for questioning, she told them that instead of harassing innocent people with all their questions, they had better find the criminals.

I was always jealous of Mário. He was always doing and getting what he wanted. My father might not approve, but in the end, he always admired Mário's guts. My father was an old-fashioned kind of Japanese. He was always talking about the true Japanese way, how in Japan children and women are obedient, about high standards and loyalty. Mário was Brazilian through and through; he didn't care about the Japanese way. Then he came to Japan and saw it was nothing like my father had said anyway. He figured the old man had left behind a Japan that didn't exist today. He told me that one day he wanted to bring our father to Japan, to see the real Japan, not the remembered Japan. But he said when the time came, he would also be a rich man. He wanted to show the old man that he had made it like a Brazilian in Japan.

I couldn't compete with Mário. I've got my faults, I'll admit. I'm not perfect. I've got a hell of a temper as Yoshiko knows well, but it's only when I drink. I don't know how to be powerful like Mário every day, all the time. I'm not like him.

When he left for Japan, I figured I'd stay behind to take care of the folks. That would be the Japanese way, like my father would appreciate, but the old man only talked about Mário, missed Mário. Sure Mário sent money home to the old man, but that was all. He left behind Cida and the kid. I felt sorry for Cida, so I went to see her. The folks never approved of her because she was a gaijin. She put up with the way they treated her and then Mário went and left her. She cried on my shoulder, and one thing led to another. That was the way it was for a long time. She cried, and one thing led to another. Yoshiko never knew. I was loyal to Yoshiko like my father would have wanted. Cida was my brother's wife. She was a good woman and didn't deserve being abandoned like that. Eventually I abandoned Cida too, left for Japan to join my brother. I had lost my job in Brazil, and he had work for me.

When I got here and saw the life he'd made for himself, saw the woman he was in love with, had to put up with his smart self-satisfied way, I wondered why I had come so far to be so humiliated. I should have stayed behind with Cida. I tore up Alice's kitchen. And just like in the old days, Mário came to find me, save me, be my brother.

Doutora

HIROSHI MATSUKAZU, A NISEI REPORTER WHO IS also a friend of mine, called to ask for a profile of the killer in this new case. We talked about some related cases of violence.

Lately in Japan, the news has been particularly shocking, not only in the Brazilian community, but in the Japanese news itself. In Kobe, there was the news of a Japanese boy who was decapitated, his head placed at the gate of his school. Until the killer was found, the Japanese news was a swirl of speculations. The most upsetting revelation was to discover that the killer was another boy, older but nevertheless a child himself.

The first time a Brazilian dekasegi made the national news was in 1992 when Terumi Maeda Junior, working in Gunma, was accused of murdering his neighbor, a young woman who worked as a hostess in a bar. Suddenly the Japanese became aware of Brazilians working in their midst, and Maeda's case gave voice to their complaints and fears about foreigners. Maeda's case was watched in Brazil as well. Brazilians interpreted the news to mean that Brazilians were poorly treated and overworked in Japan. It was assumed that stress from constant work and loneliness from being away from his family caused Maeda's act of violence. At first he confessed to the crime. Over the course of his trial, however, he would both maintain his innocence and his guilt. His confusion might have indicated schizophrenia, but without some research, I could not say for sure. In any case, Brazilian workers in Japan have long required mental health care, but we have been slow in meeting these needs. Lately, the results of our inability to provide adequate care and assistance have become painfully obvious.

In Inuyama, a Brazilian worker killed his two young children and wife. He lived in a house next to the aluminum parts factory where he worked. He threw the baby and the toddler into the furnace. Finding it difficult to haul his wife into the same furnace, he knocked on his neighbor's door and asked for help. Previous to this event, he had told a fellow worker that he was having trouble with elephants inside his house. His colleague reported this problem to the contractor in charge who unfortunately shrugged off the story.

Another horrible event involved a young Brazilian who fell in love with a woman living in the same apartment complex. When she became involved with another man, he killed that man and presented her with the dead man's arm and head.

There are also the continuing notices of suicides, assaults, indecent exposure, drug overdoses, and alcoholism leading to fights and traffic accidents. I've been aware of most of these events in a first-hand way since I handle the hotline calls designed to assist Brazilians in Japan. I don't speak to every caller; only those who request psychiatric assistance or counseling. Still, I can only talk to these people, suggest paths to assistance in

Japan or Brazil. Not being licensed in Japan, I cannot offer continued treatment or prescribe medication. Those who speak Japanese fluently can be referred to Japanese physicians; those who require Portuguese counseling might not get proper care.

Hiroshi revealed some of the details of the killing, details that were not yet written up in the newspaper reports. Both victims were stabbed several times and died from hemorrhaging and loss of blood. The killing seems to have been very messy; pieces of the victims' noses and ears and fingers were cut away. The victims were found with scant clothing, but neither were sexually abused. Their bodies were stuffed into large suitcases and left at the opening of a tunnel on the main highway. Traces of blood were found in the apartment where the couple lived. There were obvious attempts to clean away the blood. The tatami had been replaced, and a fusuma, or sliding door, had been removed. Wallpaper had also been torn away from sections of the wall.

Hiroshi said that in the beginning the police spent a great deal of time searching for the couple's missing clothing, wondering why their clothing had been removed or if they had been forced to undress. It was Hiroshi who suggested to the police that Brazilians were accustomed to sleeping in their underwear in hot weather. There was no air conditioning in the apartment, only a fan; it would have been sweltering in the summer heat. The police had wasted time speculating about weird sexual acts rather than the more logical conclusion that the killer had entered the house in the night and surprised the couple in their sleep.

Hiroshi and I speculated that the killer may not have been Brazilian. He thought a Brazilian would never use a knife, that a gun would seem to be the weapon of choice. I reminded him that a gun would be difficult to acquire in Japan. We then considered that an effort to clean up after the killing, even to hide the crime, might not be in the Brazilian mindset. It seemed odd however that anyone would think that such an event could be covered up by replacing tatami or removing anything from the apartment. Surely someone would notice. The killer didn't seem to be very experienced or to have planned his actions. The speculation that organized crime such as the yakuza was involved seemed therefore unlikely. We agreed that a member of the yakuza would have been cleaner and more premeditated in his actions, would not have left anything to chance. Hiroshi wondered if this were a crime of passion or romantic interest or one of greed and a payment of past debts. I wondered at the meaning of dispatching the bodies in suitcases left on the highway to be eventually discovered. Hiroshi suggested that the killer must have had great strength to handle the suitcases filled with dead bodies, but perhaps there had been more than one person involved in the crime. We went around and around discussing the details to produce a profile but came to no clear conclusions, whether man or woman, Brazilian or Japanese, multiple killers, psychotic, hired, vengeful, desperate.

After Hiroshi hung up, I went back to my notebooks and searched through the pages dated on the same evening of the crime. I did so merely out of curiosity. Even if I could find some connection, all of the calls were of course anonymous and confidential.

A woman called to complain about her husband and his drunken bouts of anger and destructiveness. She called because he was gone again, and she wondered if she should let him back in the house when he returned. She felt sorry for him because he was so lost in Japan, so being drunk here was even worse. She thought she might wander out into the streets and look for him. Usually she called her brother-in-law to help her, but this time she might go looking herself. Japan was so safe, even at night.

Another woman called because she feared she was being followed. She wondered if this sensation was the result of paranoia or based in reality. She couldn't be sure. Suddenly she was intermittently afraid. She had started to sleep at her boyfriend's place and sent her daughter to stay with a friend. She felt safe with her boyfriend but couldn't sleep at night worrying about her daughter. Was she crazy?

Oddly, a Japanese man also called; I had never received calls from Japanese. He explained that he had Brazilian friends but felt confused at times because of cultural misunderstandings and nuances in the language.

He often felt confused and angry even though he felt very happy with his new friends. Until he met these Brazilians, he had never felt accepted, but lately he was feeling unsure about his relationship with them. Could they really be trusted?

Finally, a man called to ask about his nightmares. Were these nightmares a sign of guilt? He had left his wife and son behind in Brazil. He was working day and night, seven days a week. He thought about nothing but making money. He sent his wife money, but he didn't want to return to her. When he got to Japan, he realized he never loved her. Recently he had fallen in love with a nisei. He wondered why he had to come to Japan to fall in love with a nisei.

In all of these cases, as usual, I mostly listened, suggested one thing or another, and, in my listening, encouraged the questioner to answer his or her own questions.

Mário

I DREAMT THAT NIGHT OF MONEY, LOTS OF MONEY. IN my dream, I opened Fátima's two enormous suitcases, the ones she brought from Brazil with all of her belongings, the ones she filled with toys and clothing for Iara and electronic goods for her family when she went back. Inside one suitcase were stacks of yen, piled the way you see money in mystery movies. In the other suitcase, stacks of American dollars were piled in the same way.

I groped around in the suitcases, touching the money, feeling the edges of the paper against my thumbs. It was tied in packages with string, nylon string like the stuff we make in the factory. I tugged at it, but the ends were knotted. I went to the kitchen and got a short but sharp knife and lifted it between the paper and the string. The string fell away easily, but in that moment a monstrous thing appeared, a hag in tattered smelly robes and long black hair. She approached me with her hair and began to wind it around my neck, choking and dragging me away. I slashed at the hair with the knife, cutting it away, but she seemed to grow more hair and wound it around me like a spider's web, entangling my arms and legs. I struggled, tearing at her garments, attacking her body with the knife. As her hands worked to weave the threads of her hair into rope, pulling and knotting it, I slashed and cut away her fingers. She screamed, and blood fell forth from her hands, coiling into red cords that spun through her hair and groped like tentacles to trap me in her embrace. I kicked and thrashed, stabbing at her breast and face, cutting away her nose and ears, blinding her, until she weakened and fell away. Still terrified with fear and madness, I hacked away the cords of her hair and blood, struggling away from that half-woven cocoon. When I finally emerged, I saw the remains of her body transformed. There, lying before me, was my wife, Cida, but as I groped toward the bloody ravaged body, the face changed, and I saw Fátima.

I awoke from this dream screaming but was immediately engulfed by a second nightmare. In the dark, a figure approached. I could not make out the features. The head was covered in a ski mask.

Marukami-san

BRAZILIANS DON'T UNDERSTAND THE NATURE OF A police investigation in Japan. Especially the Brazilian reporters. They believe that they can carry on their own investigations and publish anything they want. The police have a say in what can be published and when. This is always necessary to protect their investigation. Brazilian reporters have been overzealous in their jobs. They must feel that they have a special stake in this particular case, but they should leave it to the police. They are extremely careful and thorough. Furthermore, there are good reasons why certain information must not be divulged to the public. Japanese reporters work in concert with the police, carefully agreeing to publish only information released by official police reports. Also, Japanese reporters understand that the privacy of an individual is more important than the public's right to know. The Brazilian reporters can't understand this at all.

I have been watching these reporters going back and forth, questioning everyone, trying to find out this or that. They think they know more than the police. In some cases, because they can question their people in their own language, they must have discovered serious motives for committing the crime. If so, they should be cooperating with the police and sharing this information.

These Brazilians can be very naive. I have heard there are rumors among the Brazilians that the yakuza is involved in this crime. Brazilians believe that the contract companies are often run by the yakuza. Mário got ten of his coworkers to defect from another contractor to my contracting company. The president of the other company was furious at Mário and told him that this would end up badly for him. Mário told the contractor that late payment of salaries was not tolerable, that workers could decide for themselves what was in their best interests. Several people overheard this argument and the contractor's threat that it would end up badly for Mário. When the police interrogated these bystanders, they spoke about this threat, wondering if members of the yakuza weren't sent to kill Mário. In my opinion, this hypothesis seems absurd, based on an exaggerated desire to find a corrupt system.

I used to be the manager of a pachinko parlor. Since pachinko is a form of gambling, people also assume corruption must be involved, but it's just a business like any other. Brazilians were always hanging around at my place trying their luck with pachinko. I got friendly with some of them. Sometimes they needed a guarantor to buy a telephone connection or to rent a place. They asked me, and I always agreed to help. They spent a lot of money on pachinko, and it was good to have their business and goodwill. There were some young men who needed work, so I gave them small jobs around the parlor. They were always making jokes and enjoying life. They took me along when they went drinking or dancing. I even got a Brazilian girlfriend for a while.

I should have realized that this one young Brazilian was a bad type. He was always getting into fights. I had heard that he had stolen the motorcycle he rode around, that he made money off the sale of drugs to other Brazilians. One day, he staged an assault and robbery of the pachinko parlor. He had timed the arrival of the armored truck that carried away the day's profits and simply intercepted the metal suitcase. He got away. In fact, he was said to have escaped to Brazil. His younger brother, who was an accomplice and a rather foolish kid, was caught and interrogated. This brother suggested that I had been involved in the robbery, that I had set it up. Because of this I was also arrested. Further investigation could not prove anything against me, so I was released. It didn't matter that I was innocent. It is believed that the police are so complete and cautious in their investigations that when they arrest a person, it is because they have absolute evidence of guilt. To be arrested is equal to declaring the suspect's guilt. So, I was fired from my job. One of the newspapers wrote that I was the son of the owner, but the owner is Korean, and I'm not Korean. I was just a manager. I never made more money than a regular salary. After I lost my job, I began to wonder if it would have made better sense for me to get a cut of what the Brazilian took away.

After that, I went to work in a factory making nylon thread. That's where I met Mário. I hid my bitter feelings about my previous encounters with other Brazilians. Until then, I didn't know that some of them worked so hard, never stopping, always working overtime, especially the nisei. In the factory, I saw them compete amongst each other for overtime. No one wanted to be making less money than another, even if it meant giving up a day off to play with their children. Mário was the most aggressive of all of them. In only a few years time, he had saved a lot of money. I was surprised to learn how much. I myself had very little savings if any. Mário also had ambitious plans; he wanted his own business in Japan. The only way to make money, he said, was to be independent, to be your own boss. He wanted to start his own contracting business. He did the calculations. If he only got 100 yen per hour for each contracted worker, with ten employees, he was already making 40,000 yen a week. Every time he added ten new employees, he paid himself another 40,000 yen. The big contractors were working with over a 1,000 employees. Think of the money they were making. Mário only needed a Japanese to front for him to make the business legal. I volunteered my name.

Suddenly I was the president of my own company. Mário did most of the work, bringing new employees under our contract. I met with the owners of

123

the factories, got an idea of their needs, and assured them of our ability to fill their open positions with competent workers. One day the official papers arrived for our limited incorporation, but Mário's name was not listed as a co-owner. We had agreed that I would pretend to be the president-owner so that Mário's ex-contractor would not get suspicious as we depleted his work crew. This was just a strategy for the time being until our company became strong. Still, the official documents should include Mário's name as well. Mário became very angry. I could not convince him that it was merely a mistake. He threatened to pull his money out and find another partner.

Ana

I WAS STAKED OUT IN FRONT OF THE VICTIM'S BROTHER'S house for a week with Mara and Sônia. Mara's from the *Jornal,* and Sônia works for *Visão.* I'm with *Folha,* but I've worked for the other newspapers as well, so we're all friends from before. We decided we could save time and expenses by pooling our resources. This case was too big, and we weren't just interested in getting the scoop so much as finding out what really happened. We all had a personal interest in this case. We wanted to make sure the truth came out, make sure the Japanese didn't arrest the wrong people or find a way to cover this up.

I don't care what the Japanese police think. They've already given me an ultimatum of sorts. I wrote something they hadn't officially released for publication, and they found out. They told me if I ever did that again, I'd never get another story. The Japanese reporters agree to print only what they're allowed to by the police, but they are privy to lots of inside information. What's the point of being a spokesperson for the police? I'm one of the few Brazilian reporters who speaks and reads Japanese fluently enough to be a legal translator, so I try to go in with the Japanese reporters and share their information. One Japanese reporter was really surprised by the way we Brazilian reporters are treated by the police. Obviously there's discrimination. We aren't treated as professionals. I suppose that's why we wanted to break open this case, to show the police we could do important investigative work.

Mara, Sônia, and I took turns watching the brother's house, to see who might come or go, to catch any one of the family leaving. I went to the police station several times to see who was being interviewed. Mara did some investigating around the factory where the couple worked. We took turns going out for food and sleeping in the car. We all had our cellphones ready, communicating back and forth.

The victim's relatives wouldn't come to the door to talk to us, and when they did appear, they ran off saying that the police had prevented them from speaking to anyone. Brazilians are usually not shy about talking to us, but I also thought the brother's attitude was unfriendly and distant. I thought, his brother has died; how can he simply go about his business like this? We wondered if the family had something to hide. I began to think that they must know more. For example, Sônia found out that the brother had revealed to a co-worker that the victim, Mário, had a habit of leaving the outside porch light on when he was home. If the brother came by and the porch light was on, he'd know to visit. He'd been by the house, but since the light wasn't on, he hadn't gone in. The house had remained dark for several days, so Sérgio didn't see his brother until he had to identify his body. I suspected that whoever committed the crime knew about the porch light, knew Mário's habits. We began to think that if the brother suspected anyone, he might not be telling what he knew; he might be afraid to reveal what he knew in fear for his own life.

Sônia thought she might uncover something about the female victim, Fátima. Sônia had already been in contact with Mário's wife in Brazil. But after talking with Alice, who owns the obento business downstairs from the brother, Sônia concluded that Fátima had had a pretty hardworking routine, making pastéis for extra cash, being a single mother with no previous boyfriends or other lovers.

I went over to Mário's apartment now cordoned off by the police. Across the street was a warehouse with a guard in front. I talked to the guard who said that there's another night guard on duty as well. He's always there unless he's making rounds. Had the guards seen anything across the street? No, they were already questioned; no one had noticed anything in particular. I took pictures of the two-story house. Mário lived upstairs in one of those typical apartments with tatami, divided into two rooms by sliding doors, and a back balcony to air out the futon. I noticed that in order to remove the bodies from the apartment, someone would have had to watch for or distract the guard. Even if the bodies were lowered out of the back balcony, they would have had to be moved past the front of the house in plain sight.

Mara went off to check on the victim's bank accounts. She discovered that he had transferred a large amount of money over to his brother's account. At the same time, he shared an account with a Japanese partner named Marukami. There was a recent payment for the purchase of a car for their business and enough money to meet the next payroll. It didn't look suspicious. I went looking for Marukami who told me to leave this business to the police, who knew best. I couldn't pry him open, but then, out of the blue, I asked him if he knew about Mário's habit of leaving the porch light on. He looked shaken but then seemed to be confused by my question. Meanwhile Sônia went to a Brazilian bar where Mário and Marukami were known to meet and hang out. She got the owner to tell her that Marukami had come in one night looking very frazzled and asking if anyone had seen Mário. He sat down, saying he'd wait, and began to get drunk. Later, three other

125

Japanese friends, whom the bar owner didn't recognize, joined Marukami, drank some beers, and took him away.

On one of my rounds at the police station, I ran into Hiroshi, a fellow reporter who works for *IP*. He was a little jealous of our investigative threesome, but he said he was working on an angle, on a psychological profile of the killers. When he said killers in the plural, I realized he had also come to the conclusion that more than one were involved in the crime. Then I asked, what do you think? Brazilian, Nikkei, or Japanese? He shrugged, then said, Brazilian he's not. One down, two to go.

Fátima

HE SHOWED ME A PHOTOGRAPH OF HIS SON AT AGE three. His son is the same age as Iara, but he only has this one photograph, since he has been away from Brazil for five years now. His son and Iara are only a week apart. Iara's father was white, but she looks very much like me. No one questions whether she is Japanese or not. Mário's wife was a morena, so the boy seems to have darker features, and his hair is curly. Still, you can see Mário's smile and his eyes in the boy. I don't know how Mário can be away from his child, could have left him to never see him again. I know that he has been good to his wife in sending her money every month for all these years without fail. He says he will never stop supporting her as long as she is raising his boy. He could have simply disappeared like so many other nisei men whose photos you see in the newspapers every week. They are always the same faces. Their women and families never seem to give up looking and hoping that they'll show up. But we all know that they've taken on different names, married new women, taken up new lives. Some of them may be ashamed that they can never send any money. They may think that one day they'll reappear, successful, with lots of money, but until that time, they are "disappeared." Mário isn't like these nisei, but still I wonder about a man who doesn't need to see or be with his son. Perhaps the feelings of a mother are different.

I asked him about this several times. It's been on my mind a lot lately, and I don't want to make the wrong choices for Iara. We've been through so much together. She is my very life. In trying to explain this feeling to Mário, perhaps I made him feel guilty. Finally he became angry with my questions about his wife and child in Brazil, but I felt I had a right to know. I wanted to be sure about his feelings and my own. Instead, I think I confused him. He had to think about his marriage and his parents again. He wondered if he had married his wife to challenge his father. Since he's come to Japan, he's thought about things differently. He realizes now how much he owes his parents, how they sacrificed for him and his brother, working a small farm and selling their produce at the fairs. His father scraped all his money together to send him and his brother to school. He wanted more for his boys, but he wanted them to also continue in the

Japanese ways. Mário had nothing but scorn for his father's ways, but when he came to Japan, he realized that he and his father were the same.

I have had this sensation that someone is following me, watching me. When I turn around, there is no one there. I have been sleeping at Mário's place and leaving Iara with Alice and her children. Alice thinks my fear is crazy; she thinks it's just an excuse to sleep with Mário. How is it anyway? she asks and winks at me. She doesn't know that Mário wakes up every night in a cold sweat. He has terrible nightmares which he describes to me in great detail. Perhaps it's because of his nightmares that I have become afraid. One night while Mário was finally sleeping quietly, I thought I heard a noise and saw the shadow of a figure on the balcony. I didn't want to wake Mário who rarely sleeps so well. I went to the kitchen and quietly removed a knife which I slipped under one corner of the futon.

The Tunnel

THERE ARE SPECULATIONS THAT THE CREATION OF Japan's vast underground tunnel structures has less to do with the limitations of space or the desire to preserve the mountain environments and forests but rather to provide a vast network of shelters in case of a national emergency: earthquakes, bombs, nuclear fallout.

Two cars moving in opposite directions approached the opening of the tunnel at about the same time, one car emerging from its long darkness, the other about to enter it. The drivers, each curious to see a suitcase leaning on the side of the tunnel, stopped cautiously, got out of their cars, and hauled away the heavy suitcases, slamming the hoods of their trunks over an unknown treasure. Each of the cars then sped away into or away from the tunnel and down the highway for hundreds of kilometers, hour by hour speeding, by a computed formula, more distant from each other. At some appropriate distance, the drivers relieved their curiosities by opening the suitcases. They saw that the enormous suitcases were filled with stacks and stacks of paper money, far too much to count. One driver gasped at this sudden fortune but in any case took the entire suitcase to a police station and turned in the money, fearful that it was tainted by dishonesty. For this, the driver was rewarded with an interview on television and a small percentage of the suitcase's contents. The other driver closed the suitcase, drove to a cliff overlooking the Japan Sea, and lugging the thing with great difficulty to the edge, tossed it into the ocean.

August: Just Do It in 24 Hours

生

1997 Nike Brazil World Tour: Osaka
World Cup Exhibition Game: Brazil vs. Japan

August 13, 1997 * 7 P.M.

The preceding announcement may or may not excite your imagination depending on your attachment to soccer, to Brazil, or to the World Cup. Despite our scheduled departure from Japan on August 15, an invitation to see this game could not—I repeat—*could not* in the minds of my Brazilian husband and our son be passed up. Dunga, Ronaldo, Roberto Carlos, the coach Zagalo, Brazil's finest. They would all be there. And they would test the mettle of the new Japanese team and its aspirations to join the fury over the most contested game in the entire world.

August 13, 1 A.M.

I am awake, writing as usual as everyone else sleeps. I am doing this on the floor because we no longer have any furniture, because we are about to leave this rented house.

My friend and translator, Kenichi Eguchi, will be working as an interpreter for Nike at the exhibition game in Osaka. He has faxed us information about where to pick up free tickets and the best way to get around Osaka to the stadium. His instructions are based on taking the Shinkansen from Nagoya to Osaka, but Ronaldo has called some Brazilian friends to catch a ride. In any case, I set this information aside for Ronaldo and Jon. I putter around the last of our preparations for packing. I might under other circumstances prepare a snack for them, but we no longer have a refrigerator, not to mention food. We are living out of the Circle K convenience store in the meantime.

4 A.M.

Despite the hour, but charged over the promise of the day, Ronaldo and Jon rush out to the corner Circle K to meet our Brazilian friends. They load up with a Circle K regimen of Morinaga aloe vera juice, assorted musubis, and breads for the road.

Jorge and Masaye Takahashi pull up in a Delica van with three young men, all members of the *Viva Brasil* soccer team at Homi-Danchi. Jorge is the team captain; Masaye is the team mom. The team members are between

17 and 25; they are exemplars of the youth and energy that drive the subparts factories in and around Toyota. On weekends, these men vent their frustrations and retrieve their youth competing in traveling soccer tournaments. Today, a Wednesday, they've skipped out of their jobs in order to see live, for the first time, the Brazilian champions, the team that sustains their dreams and self-perceptions in a distant home. To lose a day of work is no small thing, but the choice is a particularly Brazilian one, steeped in a confusion of identity, rebellion, and saudades.

It's a three-hour ride over the kosoku (highway) to Osaka. It's also three hours of storytelling. There are jokes and prankster tales revealing a childhood full of a humor unimaginable in Japan or even the U.S. My son revels in the stories—escapades to steal a pizza, how to avoid radar detection when speeding, stolen car radios recycled. The stories aren't focused on dishonesty; they are told to reveal the trickster, cunning, a good joke, the stodgy made foolish, the system turned on its side. This is a world of hilarity encapsulated in a Delica van. Outside, the severe landscape, paid for by tolls at about 10 cents a kilometer, rolls out along the kosoku.

7:30 A.M.

At this early hour, they are clearly the first arrivals by car, so the Delica van gets the closest parking space to the stadium, like some kind of miracle. Its seven occupants tumble out and survey the situation. Along the sides of the stadium, people in sleeping bags have staked their claims overnight to places in a long winding line of fans, hopeful of getting the choice seats in general admission. Two of the young Brazilians take off to scout the stadium, slipping through the gates, wandering through the empty stands, making use of the bathrooms, taking photographs like accomplished spies.

8:45 A.M.

Ronaldo meets Kenichi at the appointed time and place and receives the four coveted tickets to the game. The story is that this game sold out months ago in the first hour of sales, so the value of these tickets is compounded by the moment. Scalpers with wads of cash buy and sell, offering a $40 ticket for as much as $150. The Delica crew needs three more tickets, but $150 is too high.

10 A.M.

Ronaldo and Jon make a run for McMuffins at McDonald's. The crew scarfs down three apiece. Some children have a ball and are playing soccer. The Brazilians are soon playing with the kids.

Masaye has spread out a mat to sit; some nod off to nap.

NOON

The concession booths begin to open, stalls selling food and soccer paraphernalia. Other Brazilians gather in bunches, their carousing and jocular repartee evident.

They sport the soccer shirts of their home teams, dozens of local affiliations. A Japanese man with missing teeth appears with a bag full of J-League soccer shirts which he proudly displays one by one, his personal collection, all his local affiliations. It's a meeting of minds, and soon he is trying to learn Brazilian songs and is yelling Brazilian slogans.

Meanwhile a group of Japanese women has already joined the festivities, gamely trying to learn the Dança da Garrafa. It's a lewd dance, its raunchy movements swaying and pumping over a strategically placed Coke bottle. The Brazilian men demonstrate a few steps. The Japanese women follow along in good humor. Things are getting heated up.

1 P.M.

About this time, large booster groups are being ushered into a second inner courtyard beyond the gates. These special fans are in lines, getting their special booster tickets. One of the Delica crew slips into this line, pretends to be part of the group, and scores a ticket. Each ticket is encased lovingly in a plastic cover with special shoelaces that allow you to wear it like a necklace. Moreover, special stamps are glued to the cover indicating the booster status of the bearer. One ticket down; two to go.

Suddenly the rest of the booster group invades the scene with large flags, and three of the Delica crew find themselves swept through the gates into the stadium. They pull away from the crowd and gain access to the

inside of the stadium itself. Sneaking in and out of bathrooms, wending their way to the top of the stadium, hiding in the stands, they communicate all the while between themselves and their friends outside the stadium with cellphones. "We are in the bathroom on the north side." "We are now at the top of the stands above the reserved section." "There's a security guard at the south door. Cuidado!" It's Mission Impossible.

2 P.M.

By this time, the security guards have caught the three crew members and kicked them out, but not without causing some commotion between the guards themselves, some of whom are reprimanded by superiors for allowing this situation to occur. However, the young man with the special booster ticket and stamps is allowed to stay.

Cellular phone calls reach out to Brazilians on the road approaching Osaka. Someone has scored some tickets for this group; they are on their way. But they get into an accident. No one is hurt, but the car is totaled. They abandon it, rent another, and arrive at the stadium. No one is going to miss this game.

3 P.M.

Masaye overhears three Japanese girls talking about friends who haven't arrived. They have two extra tickets. The three Japanese girls are quickly taken in by the Delica crew. Suddenly they are part of a Brazilian thing. The joviality of the young men, their easy banter and friendly joshing surround the girls like a tropical beach. For one day, they are *in* Brazil. There is nothing in the world, short of being in Brazil, that can match this. The girls agree to sell their extra tickets at cost. That's it. The two final tickets. Seven Brazilians. Seven tickets.

5 P.M.

Things are intensifying at the front. A samba group is drumming it up. Brazilians can't be without their rhythms. The noisy ruckus and hilarity are infectious. The sensation of it swells with expectation.

The crew member with the special booster ticket gets in early with the designated fan club. He moves in quickly and stakes out fifteen choice seats at the very front of general admission. There are places for all his old and new friends, including the three Japanese girls. The folks back in line packing up their sleeping bags never had a chance.

Nike is passing out Nike fans, Nike stickers, and Nike face tattoos. No doubt there are Nike hats, Nike shirts, and Nike buttons. This is a Nike World Event. The crew gets in line for the freebies. They get some, pass them out, get in line again, get some more.

Ronaldo and Jon move to their reserved seats, but the hoopla is definitely back in general admission with the Brazilian samba band and the Delica crew's trickster ways.

6 P.M.

There is a capoeira and samba show before the game starts as well as a taiko show.

The game happens. It's 1 to 0, Brazil over Japan, at halftime. During the first half, a Brazilian is seen running onto the field to shake hands with the players on the team. It's all on international TV. The man is ushered off the field and kicked out.

During halftime, Ronaldo and Jon rejoin the partying crew in general admission. The three Japanese girls are trying to learn the Dança da Garrafa.

Second half. 3 to 0, Brazil. Neither Ronaldo nor Jon will later remember who made the goals. The steam of Brazilian revelry that filled the very air gradually seeps away. The rhythms tire. The carnival reveals its tristeza.

10 P.M.

Later, the Brazilian who was seen running onto the field is met by his friends. He shrugs off having missed the second half. He had run onto the field to be on international television, and was certain that his family in Brazil must have seen him. For the moment, he is exuberant with his success. At midnight, he will turn back into a dekasegi.

The three Japanese girls who have attached themselves to the Delica crew hang on to their last moments with Brazil. One girl bursts into tears as they leave.

The crew piles into the Delica, pulls out of Osaka, taunting banter filling the van. "Hey Jon, you made that girl cry. What did you have to do that for?" Shy and fifteen, he's the youngest. They slap him across the head. "Loverboy!" He's one of the crew. Then everything settles into the light snoring of sleeping men. Three hours back again to Nagoya.

1 A.M.

Back at the Circle K. I'm up writing as usual. The guys fill our now-empty rented place with their still-high energy and wild sense of excess, an excess that has little to do with the game they have struggled for the past 24 hours so valiantly to see. My questions: How was the game? What was the score? Who made a goal? All irrelevant.

7 Brazilians went 24 hours and 250 kilometers with only the hope of seeing a soccer game that had been sold out months in advance. What could they lose but a chance to test their ingenuity, their infallible charm, their cunning, their facility to play? This was the game at hand. At midnight, as the Delica churned its engine across the highway, they must have stirred in their old roles; peons they would call themselves, dekasegi. No matter. At one o'clock, a wild sense of excess, the trickster's success, momentary but marvelous havoc, filled our house one last time in Seto, Japan.

Saudade

A Brazilian friend has said that saudade is a word that cannot be translated, only approximated: longing, homesickness, nostalgia. In English it would seem to mean a longing for home, for the familiar that is distant and out of reach. A long way from Brazil, you can feel or have saudade for a song by João Gilberto, for Dadá's seafood muqueca, for the salty humidity that crinkles your hair, for the easy embrace of old friendships. But Brazilians also express saudade for things within reach. How can we miss what is here at hand, here to touch and to caress? Gigeta, an Italian immigrant to Brazil and the great-grandmother to our children, explained it thus: Saudade, she said, is the feeling you have when you greet a waking child. What could she have meant to say about this tender moment when you forgive a child all those naughty and irritating hours awake, coax her from a dream of flight or yank him from a nightmare, seeking the embrace that renews tired bones and knocks you out of

your selfish adulthood? Here in the ephemeral present resides a complicated net of sensations: joy for life, sadness for time passing, hope for the future. Saudade.

I think there is a similar word in Japanese: natsukashii. Translation to English is similarly approximating: dear, beloved, old, nostalgic. Claude Lévi-Strauss, when explaining his saudade for Brazil, spoke of another Japanese word, awa-re, meaning sorrow and pathos. I wonder if these words evoke the same complicated net of sensations that resonate effortlessly as a bossa nova that lingers in your mind's ear. Do you also nurse a constant lump in your throat, a tightness around your heart, a breathlessness full of wonder and fear?

Saudade would seem to be a sweet sickness, but when Brazilians speak of it, they often use the expression *matar a saudade,* which means literally, *to kill* saudade. If, for example, a Brazilian has recently returned from visiting his home, he might be asked if this trip were enough to kill his saudades. Deu para matar a saudade? In some sense you must do battle with your yearning, a monster in your path. At the same time, to kill saudade is a delicious violence, a succumbing to desire, Carnaval's brief bacchanal.

Perhaps such a circling definition is still too simple, for saudade is made possible and complex by memory. What is the memory that has traveled with saudade? Saudade probably embarked from Portugal, the teary adeus to the sailor off to navigate the world. There goes Magalhães. There goes Cabral. Discover the world, but come home to me, to Lisboa, to Oporto. We will not forget you. We will hold saudades for you. Some saudades remained at home, and some saudades departed on a ship with the Portuguese sailor and traveled across the world to Brazil. But when it arrived, it became transformed, transformed by the imagination of a New World, untouched and innocent. In this, saudade became also a part of an encounter with wonder, an intense sensation of awe at the unbelievable. This is not to ignore all the blood and guts spilled in the name of that awe, that imagination; the blood and guts happened because of and for saudade. The sailor who turned settler announced: I will transform this land into my home in order not to suffer saudade. Yet he suffered anyway, and his saudade in its transformation never quite returned home to Portugal.

If the Portuguese brought the word *saudade*, others came to add their special interpretations: African slaves, Dutch traders, New Christians, Confederate soldiers, Spanish, Italians, Germans, Syrians, Japanese. Every new community came to redefine saudade for another layer of memory and belief. Africans contributed their word *banzo*, translated as a deadly melancholy, but also as daydreaming, and sorrowful, depressed, pensive, pondering. By the time Claude Lévi-Strauss arrived in Brazil, saudade was perhaps what he sensed as he defined the sad tropics, that nostalgia for a future that eludes our grasping, for a home that is at every moment in the process of extinction. Later, another anthropologist, Roberto da Matta, would describe saudade in relationship to a fluid rather than chronological understanding of time. Saudade, as a collective memory of a premodern past, stands in the way of embracing order and progress and official histories and is perhaps antimodern in its improvisation of a song or intimate poem, an enchanted invocation to stay the inevitable passage of time. Saudade links the past to the present and lives in the magical reality of daily life. Nowadays, however, landless peasants and indigenous people contest the saudade that romanticizes their poverty and extinction, the saudade that has infected Brazil like the common cold, a memory of the future embedded inside someone else's past.

Saudade continues to travel. Japanese immigrants, like the others, have absorbed saudade and, like the sailor, have transformed it for themselves. Their children carry it in their blood, under their skin, behind their eyeballs, set in their teeth, carry it now across an airborne route to the other end of the Old World. Saudade has arrived in Japan. Who can say how saudade may be again transformed as it meets natsukashii and awa-re and travels into another realm of imagination and memories —other imaginations of desire, innocence, and savagery, other memories of extinction and the future? What blood and guts? What saudade must be killed to belong, to make a home, to realize desire?

Samba Matsuri

新

Oizumi Oriente Para o Mundo

Oi oi oi Oizumi
Sol nascente maior
Grande fonte de alegria
Despertar da fantasia
Para a vida bem melhor

Neste trem bala, nosso sonho a desfilar carnaval
Carnaval, matsuri, samurais, guaranis
Renderão ao se iluminar neste mantra leme e lume
Oração que a paz resume
E que nos une em ti Oizumi, Oi Oizumi

—SAMBA BY WALTER KURODA

COUPLE # ① Nikkei to Não-Nikkei

Marcolina married a nisei because she was always fascinated by Japanese culture. As a young girl growing up in Brazil, she collected Japanese bric-a-brac. Her room was completely decorated with Japanese pictures and artifacts. She slept under calendar photographs of Mount Fuji, cherry blossoms, and rocks tied together with rope. She liked to take the bus to the Liberdade and spend the afternoon in the Japanese curio shops looking at the dolls dressed in kimonos, selecting fans, and collecting origami paper. She believed that in another life she must have been Japanese, maybe even a geisha. All her friends were nisei, and she learned to eat with ohashi.[1] She loved to go to their homes and eat Japanese food. Sukiyaki was her favorite meal. Of course, when it came time to date, she always preferred the Japanese boys.

After she got married to Paulo she learned to cook Japanese food. She also studied flower arranging. Paulo never cared about Japanese culture the way she did. He couldn't understand her interest in dressing up the kids like Japanese for obon, but he went along with it. He thought she just wanted to impress his parents.

When Paulo lost his job, it was Marcolina who insisted that they go to Japan. She didn't have any problem

---

[1] chopsticks

leaving Brazil. When she got to Japan, she adapted very quickly and learned enough Japanese to get around. She started a child care center in her home, then moved to a rented place.

Now she's making good money and has a good reputation among Brazilian mothers. Paulo works all day and sometimes nights in a factory painting batteries for Toyota cars. He wears a face mask to filter out the fumes and the fine paint spray. Sometimes he forgets to remove the mask and wears it home. He thinks only about the day when he can return to Brazil. Every year he tells Marcolina that they should be leaving next year, but Marcolina loves Japan. She loves her life here. She finds it safe for her children, and she appreciates the education they are getting. She likes the clean streets and the organization. She likes the rules and the traditions. She likes the stable economy and the fact that you can depend on the prices to be the same. She likes the way people are polite. She never wants to leave. She'll keep things rolling along so that every year, there will always be one more year.

COUPLE # ② Nikkei to Nikkei

Mariko and João never dated other Nikkei in Brazil.

Mariko found nisei men unattractive and authoritarian. She would never date a nisei; that was her unspoken rule. Maybe her parents would have liked her to date nisei, but she had a mind of her own about this. Maybe she was rebelling; she didn't know.

João never thought much about nisei girls. He was used to dating gaijin. He didn't know what race his girlfriends were. One had an Italian background. They were just Brazilians. It never occurred to him to look for a nisei. Maybe his parents would have liked his girlfriends to be Japanese, but they never said anything. When he saw a nisei woman, he didn't get terribly excited, or even interested enough to get her phone number or anything like that. He thought they weren't his type.

Mariko came to Japan married to a non-Nikkei. After they arrived, they fought constantly. He became impossibly dependent on her, as though because she was nisei, she should handle all their problems and take care of every situation. She got tired of taking care of him. Suddenly, a grown man was reduced to a child. She lost respect for him completely. They finally decided to separate. Mariko thought her husband would return to 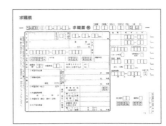 Brazil, but instead he wanted to stay anyway. She agreed to continue to be married to him, on paper, so that he could remain in Japan. Later he told her he was dating a "real" Japanese woman. She's waiting for him to marry the real Japanese so that she can divorce him.

João left a girlfriend behind in Brazil. He had told her he would return in a few years, but after a while, she wrote him to say she couldn't wait any longer. She had found someone else. Even though he remembered that she was one of the most beautiful women he had ever dated, he found it strange that he couldn't really remember her face.

After a couple of years in Japan, like other nisei, both Mariko and João had found themselves in a strange limbo. When in Brazil, they were always called japonês; now in Japan, the Japanese treated them as foreigners, wrote their names in katakana. Who were they? And yet when Mariko and João met, a sudden recognition passed between them. Perhaps it was love.

COUPLE # ③ Nikkei to Mattaku Nihonjin

Marcos Kubo came to Japan because he had never been there before. He had been all over Brazil, worked as a musician in Rio, sold his paintings in São Paulo, mined for gold in Rondonia, worked as a computer consultant in Recife. In the Americas, he had farmed on a cooperative in Cuba, played soccer in Peru, fished in Chile. He had also been to Europe, followed the grape harvest in southern France, worked in a sausage factory in Germany, took night classes in London. Along the way, he had girlfriends, a wife, and even a kid. Somehow they all got left behind as he passed on to the next country or the next job. Marcos was a man in constant movement, a man on a journey without a destination. Signing up to go to Japan was his gateway to Asia.

During six years in Japan, he had nine different jobs. Sure he was a man on the move in charge of his own time, but in Japan, not keeping his job was always caused by one problem or another. At the first job he had to work a machine he'd never seen in his life. No one came around to show him how it worked; he started experimenting to see what it could do. A manager-type came out and yelled at him: Baka![2] Well, Marcos didn't know much Japanese, but he knew baka, so he shook his head and said: Baka, não. But the manager kept yelling at him and wouldn't take the baka back. So Marcos started to run at him with a pipe, cursing the manager with every Japanese and Brazilian cuss word he knew, including a bunch he invented on the spot. Other workers intervened, but he had to leave that job the first day.

A secretary in the office who witnessed the incident wondered about this stranger who fearlessly confronted the manager, known for his gross and autocratic manner. Maybe she also wondered about some of those invented cuss words. She followed Marcos out of the factory, never to return. Perhaps Yoko had an intuition about

---

[2] fool, idiot, stupid

BEM-VINDO AO JAPÃO.
A FORÇA DO SEU TRABALHO SERÁ BEM-VINDA NO JAPÃO.

BEM-VINDO AO BRASIL.
O RESULTADO DO SEU TRABALHO SERÁ BEM-VINDO NO BRASIL.

Marcos. Certainly she had a curiosity and a kind of relief that her world, which seemed so predictable and mundane, could after all be different, spontaneous, invented. She joined Marcos on his journey, a journey she would also make her own.

Marcos and Yoko began to work and travel through Japan. After Japan, awaits the world.

Samba Matsuri

By some act of providence, or fiction, couple #1: Marcolina and Paulo, couple #2: Mariko and João, and couple #3: Yoko and Marcos, were all there, together, at the Samba Matsuri. Reporter Hiroshi Matsukazu, however, had no interest in following their stories. He, like a happy puppy dog, was trailing after the gorgeous and very charming Miss Nikkei, Mônica Sakamoto. She was wearing Brazilian designer jeans, Brazilian shoes, and a Nike World Cup T-shirt with a

サンバ、ランバダ、サルサ
SAMBA、LAMBADA、SAUSA

photo of the Brazilian champions silk-screened across and molded to her perfect breasts. In fact everything seemed molded to her statuesque beauty: the Brazilian flag patched to the back right pocket of her bumbum, her golden tan, her glorious smile. Hiroshi practically followed her into the dressing room where she slipped into a sequined green and gold gown and emerged a radiant queen.

Meanwhile, Marcolina was dressing up in white lace and a matching turban. She had made a

matching outfit for her little girl, and flared green and yellow silk pants for her boy. She handed her son a tambourine and applied lipstick to her daughter's lips. "Okay, children. Get ready to dance!"

This year three escola de sambas were competing for first place: JaBrasil, Unidos d'Oizumi, and JaPortela. Marcolina hummed the tune of the samba for JaBrasil and bustled out with her brood. She could see Paulo staring in the  same direction as the crowd. They were all watching Miss Nikkei climb into the shiny Miata convertible. "What are you looking at?" she queried him when she got close enough.

"That Miss Nikkei, of course," he smiled. Then he sneered, "If she's Nikkei, then you're a baiana."

"I *am* a baiana," Marcolina pouted, adjusting her turban and the flounce on the skirt of her Afro-Brazilian costume. "Don't we look good?"

"You look wonderful, but it's one thing to pretend to be a baiana and another to pretend to be Nikkei."

"Pretend to be Nikkei?"

"Yeah, I'm willing to bet that Miss Nikkei doesn't have a drop of Japanese blood. Did anyone consult her koseki tohon?[3] What a fake!"

"What do you care if she's a fake? You're just like every other man here, interested in her butt."

---

[3] certified family register (necessary to prove Japanese ancestry)

"Well, let's look at her butt. No Nikkei has a butt like that. I say if you're going to be Miss Nikkei, you have to be Nikkei."

"Why are you being so picky all of a sudden?"

By this time, others in the crowd had become interested in the argument. "He's right," someone agreed. "I have more Japanese in the nail of my little finger than she has in her entire body."

"Yeah, but what a body!" someone chimed in. "No one-hundred-percent Nikkei could ever put together a body like that."

Another put in his opinion. "You want beauty, you have to cheat! You have to mix up the bloodlines. Beautiful women are all mestiças."

"But," yelled Paulo over the crowd, "that woman is not mestiça with Japanese blood, I tell you. So she can't be Miss Nikkei!"

"What nonsense," Marcolina quipped. "You might be Nikkei, but I've got more Japanese culture running through these veins than you'll ever have."

"What are you defending her for," Paulo was screaming by now. "You wouldn't be here if it weren't for me. It's my blood that counts. And since I've been here I've been giving my blood for you." He pushed his palms forward to show his wrists.

Marcolina rolled her eyes at the invisible stigmata. "Looks like you still have all your fingers."

At that, one man thrust his hand in Marcolina's face to show her his missing indicator. "Look at this. This is what I sacrificed in coming here," he railed at her and the growing crowd. All around them JaBrasil was trying to assemble themselves.

Marcolina shouted after her children running in circles around the drumming unit, which was warming up.

The man without his finger shouted above the rising beat. He pointed with his invisible finger at Miss Nikkei waiting in the convertible for her turn to be escorted down the ogling avenue. "That woman is an offense to my sacrifice!"

Then someone came between Marcolina and the man. "How do you know she hasn't got some Nikkei in her?" he asked. "Maybe you left your finger up her ass!" to which the crowd, enthused by the rhythms, shots of pinga, and the continuing argument, roared in laughter.

In response, the man curled his remaining fingers into a tight fist and slammed it into the joker's chin. The scuffle spread among the revelers. Marcolina ran after her children and scurried away from the fracas, turning back only to see a bewildered Miss Nikkei sitting alone in the throne of her Miata surrounded by a riot of punching and kicking men and women. One man was thrown across the hood of the car. Hiroshi, who had been leaning against the car trying to get points in with Miss Nikkei, shoved the fighters out of the way, jumped into the driver's seat, and tried to gun the car and its queen through the melee. As the police ran into the crowd with sticks, the Miata slipped away to safety. For some reason, a portion of the escola de samba remembered its purpose, the beating drums calling its members to attention, and the fight choreographed its way appropriately into a reveling street perfor-

TOYOTAPÍA

mance. Miss Nikkei, saved, was nonetheless disheveled and sweaty, her makeup dripping down her frightened face. Oblivious to her distress, the great ocean of dancing humanity, much of it naked and feathered, squeezed past her majesty and into the narrow corridor of this Japanese parade.

Hiroshi went off to find a drink machine and returned with a can of Pokari Sweat. "Don't worry about missing the parade," he reassured her, popping the top of the sports drink and handing it to her. "The crowning on the stage in the afternoon is more important and certainly more dignified."

At that moment, Mariko ran up to them. "Where can I find the police?" she asked anxiously.

"Probably following the riot in that parade," Hiroshi pointed down the street.

"A man's been beaten up very badly," Mariko insisted.

"We know all about it. We had front row seats."

"What do you mean? It was back there two blocks in a narrow alleyway. There were a dozen of them. My boyfriend is with the guy, but what if they come back? He'll get hurt too." Mariko was getting frantic.

"Okay, okay," Hiroshi nodded. "I'll be right back." He patted Miss Nikkei on the shoulder.

When Mariko arrived with Hiroshi, there was already a crowd of people either staring or trying to offer assistance. Even with his face bloodied, Hiroshi recognized the young man on the ground. He was the son of one of the community leaders. Rumor had it that he was also the head of a gang of young heavies who enjoyed getting into fights. He and his friends were extorting money from shopkeepers in return for a little "protection," to prevent fights in their establishments. Since his father looked the other way, nothing could be done. It seemed that a few people had decided to take matters into their own hands. This was a story Hiroshi had been eager to verify. He flipped open his notepad and forgot about Miss Nikkei.

Mariko ran over and huddled with João over the beaten man. They spoke quickly to Hiroshi, confirming details of the incident, while the poor broken man, agreeing or disagreeing, spoke incoherently through broken teeth.

142

In the meantime, Miss Nikkei looked at her watch. What had happened to her escort? And what about the reporter covering the event? Everyone had abandoned her. She got out of the car. Her high heels and slim gown confined her steps, but she slowly made her way through the crowd. She could see a platform raised as a stage in a green area of a park. As she approached it, she could hear Japanese spoken over the loudspeakers. It didn't matter what language, speeches always sounded like speeches. Dignitaries were seated in chairs on the stage. She could see her Japanese counterpart, Miss Matsuri, seated onstage too, and next to her was an empty chair. Miss Nikkei hurried to occupy her place. No one protested; they politely nodded as she took her seat.

ひとりひとりを考えて　5つの爽快シャワー

What Miss Nikkei did not know was that the Samba Matsuri was divided into two festivals, the Brazilian and the Japanese, the Samba and the Matsuri, oil and water. Therefore, on another platform, at the other end of the park, the Samba end, the Brazilian community was also enacting formalities with a similar series of speeches. Commercial sponsors, politicians, and consular attachés all rose to the occasion, despite the intense afternoon heat and the debilitating humidity. In the final moments, when Miss Nikkei was called upon for her triumphant crowning, a small band of musicians held forth on the flourish while the master of ceremonies paused with dramatic anticipation.

When Miss Nikkei did not appear, the crowd began to boo. Marcos, a musician in the band, looked out on the crowd. He didn't appreciate the booing. Boo, não, he announced. As it happened, Marcos and the other members of the band were costumed in drag. Yoko had created his exotic costume, a red silk gown padded with balloons, on the inside as well as the outside. Marcos ran to the front of the stage in exaggerated ecstasy, waving to the crowd and pressing his hands to his cheeks, while Yoko jumped onto the stage and followed all his movements with her Nikon. The master of ceremonies shrugged and decided to crown Marcos to great cheers from the crowd. The rest of the band sidled up to the front with their instruments and arranged themselves like a court around their queen.

Meanwhile, Miss Nikkei was following suit. When Miss Matsuri got up and bowed to the Japanese crowd, so did she.

☺

That evening, August's full moon rose in the clear skies, the shimmer from its light a slight respite in the dark-but-heated air of the night. Recorded music, alternating in Japanese obon and Brazilian samba, blared from speakers off a makeshift tower in the center of the park. Circling the tower, dancers moved beneath the soft glow of colorful paper lanterns suspended from a web of electric wires. Miss Nikkei, who had returned to the comfort and anonymity of her jeans, sat on a park bench with the reporter, Hiroshi Matsukazu, who listened to the story of her humiliating day and apologized profusely.

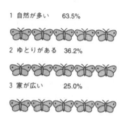

Marcolina and her children were appropriately attired in yukata and wooden geta. Paulo followed them around morosely, his left eye bandaged, the purple bruise hidden by the night. When the children ran off with money to buy shaved ice, the couple sidled together reluctantly. "Maybe next year this time, we'll be in São Paulo," Paulo suggested.

"Maybe." Marcolina answered and squeezed his hand.

Nearby João and Mariko shared dango on a stick. Mariko whispered into João's ear. "I'm pregnant," she announced.

Unlike the other Nikkei in the crowd, too shy or bored to dance, 先祖 Marcos and Yoko never stopped dancing. They danced all the Japanese folk dances, the samba, the bottle dance, and the macarena. They danced with pleasure and abandon. They danced all night.

Epilogue: Wagahai wa Nikkei de Aru

者

NATSUME SOSEKI'S FAMOUS NOVEL, *WAGAHAI wa Neko de Aru,* is told through the eyes of an imperious cat who watches his master struggle with a changing world. A translation of the title to *I Am a Cat* cannot convey its full meaning; the first person use of *wagahai* is not only archaic but reserved for a king. Borrowing from Soseki, thus, *Wagahai wa* Nikkei *de Aru.*

I have been consulting my genealogy and have discovered that I come from a continuous family line from the Gifu area extending back to the 1700s. In fact I represent the thirteenth generation. All these years they have been trying to pass me off as a sansei, but indeed I am a *jusansei.* Some may doubt it, but I am a mattaku[1] *complete* Nikkei. They

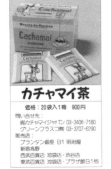

カチャマイ茶

価格: 20袋入1箱 900円

問い合せ先:
㈱カチャマイジャパン 03-3406-7180
グリーンプラスコ㈱ 03-3707-6290
販売店:
ブランタン銀座 B1 明治屋
新宿高野
西武百貨店 池袋店・渋谷店
東武百貨店 池袋店・プラザ館B1階

KAREN TEI YAMASHITA

point to my frizzier hair or the lack of an epicanthic fold in my eyelids. A hybrid, they mutter. Let them talk. The lineup of my antecedents is purely Japanese. Hey, I have a written genealogy to prove it.

Now my husband is a mattaku gaijin. Mattaku gaijin don't need genealogies to prove anything. They are just non-Nikkei. Nikkei or non-Nikkei. This is important especially if you are a dekasegi since you can only get into Japan to work based on your relative proximity to Nikkeiness. The importation of our breed is guaranteed by

CLASSIFICADO SAI

Nome:
Descendência Japonesa: Sim ( )Issei ( ) Nissei ( )Sansei
Não, casado(a) com( )Issei ( ) Nissei ( )Sansei
Tempo de visto: _____ anos. Idade:_____ Sexo: _____
Outro tipo de visto _____
Data de nascimento: ___/___/___
Telefone ou endereço para contato:

Observações:

Gibo Company: Ebisu Bldg, 304, 1-8-14 Ebisu, Shibuya-Ku, Tokyo 150

immigration laws and gives us the privilege of working legally. Nikkeiness. Don't you just love being Nikkei? You get that warm fuzzy feeling all over. I am a Nikkei. Ooouu, yummy. Taste of shoyu on your tongue. Nisei Week. Obon. A Colônia. A little bunka, see? Pound the mochi come oshogatsu. Garantido.

The food, the culture, okay, but, geographically speaking, what exactly makes a Nikkei? For example, if you are born in Japan, go to the Americas and live, maybe even forget your Japanese language, then come back, are you Nikkei? Or if you go and come back, learn Portuguese but don't forget your Japanese, and become an empreiteira and make scads of money off the dekasegi, are you Nikkei?

---

1 entirely, completely

Hey, what's Alberto Fujimori? I mean, if he's not Peruvian, is he Nikkei? What about if you pay 500 reais and get adopted into the Sakamoto family? Or if you get an eye job and a fake passport? I heard a rumor that the imperial family came centuries ago from Korea. And there are plenty of books suggesting that the original Japanese are a lost tribe from Israel. Speaking of tribes, I thought the literal translation of Nikkei is "of the Japanese tribe," but "real" Japanese never refer to themselves as Nikkei. So who's Nikkei?

My kids are Nikkei. I'll say that much, but they're not mattaku. They can't just disappear into the background and pretend to be real Japanese. Of course we Nikkei can always spot other Nikkei, mattaku or not. You see us pretending to sleep

on trains or flipping through the magazines at the kon-bini; don't be mistaken, we are always watching you. Sometimes being a Nikkei can be a disappearing act; we can become invisible. But, some of us seem to be actually self-destructing, losing parts of our bodies—fingers and arms, even heads, for example. Some go in for suicide and poof, they're ashes.

As for my kids, their Eurasian features are a dead giveaway. They have big beautiful eyes like all the Japanese cartoon characters. Their beauty is the occidental beauty that Japanese dream of, isn't it? Look at all the Miss Nikkei; who among them is mattaku Nikkei? Can a mattaku Nikkei be beautiful? What is beauty in a place where it is preferable to be the same? What is beauty when your features and gestures seem to change with your food, the very climate and social response of your home?

And where is home? Lately Nikkei seem to have several homes. Some Nikkei have more than one family, not to mention more than one wife, husband, or lover. It gets lonely on the other side of the world, KDD, ITJ, IDC, and callback notwithstanding. A voice on the line in a place where the weather is hot when you are freezing cold and cold when you are beyond hot cannot be satisfying. Suddenly you have a vision of yourself—another Nikkei—cold when you are cold, hot when you are hot. You would have never dated a Nikkei back home. Never. Now among the crowds of Japanese women all dressed in the latest lime and orange polyester, this Nikkei looks attractive. Now, while you work robotically through the day's kensa, that Nikkei in the oily uniform working the heavy machinery looks attractive. Now. Home is where you are hot and cold together.

So now we've got Nikkei getting together to make more Nikkei. Half of the kids born in Oizumi these days are Brazilian. What is the world coming to? We're procreating like rabbits! That is, we're procreating like Nikkei. Maybe the next generation can answer or reject these questions, unless they grow up illiterate. They could grow up Japanese, get domesticated and all, but the documents will prove they're not. Being born in Japan doesn't necessarily have any meaning other than the labor of it. Some Nikkei are biding their time; one or two more years and they can get a Japanese passport. That might be a ticket to somewhere: Canada, Australia, America. Or just going home, wherever that is. Japan might not be the final resting place.

Nikkei on the move. I might meet you on a train in Bangladesh, a marketplace in Algiers, a sauna in Stockholm, atop a mesa in Hopi country, online at *CaféCreole*. I'll say Wagahai wa Nikkei de aru. Are you?

調 和

想像

OTHER TITLES BY KAREN TEI YAMASHITA

Through the Arc of the Rain Forest

"Yamashita presents a critique of human waste and stupidity that is fluid and poetic as well as terrifying." —NEW YORK TIMES BOOK REVIEW

"Bizarre and baroque, funny and sad. Karen Tei Yamashita's novel may say more about saving the rain forest that its nonfiction counterparts do." —UTNE READER

$12.95 / novel / 0-918273-82-x / paper

Brazil-Maru

"The publication of Brazil-Maru establishes Karen Tei Yamashita as one of the significant new voices in American Fiction. Brazil-Maru is a deceptively corrosive tale of betrayal and self-deception that has particular relevance to the shattered world that we all inhabit." —PAUL YAMAZAKI, CITY LIGHTS BOOKSELLERS

$19.95 / novel / 1-56689-000-4 / cloth 12.95 / novel / 1-56689-016-0 / paper

Tropic of Orange

"A big talent." —THE LOS ANGELES TIMES

Irreverently juggling magical realism, film noir, hip hop, and chicanismo, Karen Tei Yamashita presents an L.A. where the homeless, gangsters, infant organ entrepreneurs, and Hollywood collide on a stretch of highway struck by disaster. The Harbor Freeway crisis becomes the apex of events—caused by an orange, which has been brought to L.A. from just north of Mazatlan, dragging with it the Tropic of Cancer.

$14.95 / novel / 1-56689-064-0 / paper

COFFEE HOUSE PRESS

THE ENGLISH COFFEE HOUSE of the 1600s was a place of fellowship where ideas were freely exchanged. The Parisian cafés of the early 1900s witnessed the birth of dadaism, cubism, and surrealism. The American coffee house of the 1950s, a refuge from conformity for beat poets, exploded with literary energy.

This spirit lives on in the pages of Coffee House Press books.

Good books are brewing at coffeehousepress.org.

COLOPHON

Circle K Cycles was designed at Coffee House Press
in the Warehouse District of downtown Minneapolis.
The text is set in Gill Sans.